The

CHRISTMAS
TREE FARM

Books by Melody Carlson

The
CHRISTMAS TREE FARM

A Christmas Novella

MELODY CARLSON

Revell

a division of Baker Publishing Group
Grand Rapids, Michigan

Published by Revell
a division of Baker Publishing Group
Grand Rapids, Michigan
RevellBooks.com

Printed in the United States of America

Library of Congress Cataloging-in-Publication Data
Names: Carlson, Melody, author.
Title: The Christmas tree farm : a Christmas novella / Melody Carlson.
Description: Grand Rapids, Michigan : Revell, a division of Baker Publishing Group, 2024.
Identifiers: LCCN 2024006005 | ISBN 9780800744724 (cloth) | ISBN 9781493447114 (ebook)
Subjects: LCSH: Christmas tree growing—Fiction. | Family farms—Fiction. | LCGFT: Christmas fiction. | Romance fiction. | Christian fiction. | Novellas.
Classification: LCC PS3553.A73257 C57 2024 | DDC 813/.54—dc23/eng/20240216
LC record available at https://lccn.loc.gov/2024006005

This book is a work of fiction. Names, characters, places, and incidents are the product of the author's imagination or are used fictitiously. Any resemblance to actual events, locales, or persons, living or dead, is coincidental.

Jacket illustration: Nate Eidenberger
Jacket design: Laura Klynstra

Baker Publishing Group publications use paper produced from sustainable forestry practices and postconsumer waste whenever possible.

24 25 26 27 28 29 30   7 6 5 4 3 2 1

1

The pungent smell of damp burnt wood stung Madison McDowell's nostrils even before she opened her Jeep door. She glumly shook her head as she took in the vicious devastation of what used to be the loveliest section of the McDowell's Family Christmas Tree Farm. She zipped her fleece jacket to hold off the stiff autumn breeze whipping across the rippling river. Sadly, there was even more wildfire damage on the other side of the water. The once-valuable Douglas fir timber growing straight up the side of the steep ravine was now reduced to row after row of blackened skeletal poles. Were they even salvageable? The fast-flowing water was strewn with fallen trees from both sides. A good habitat for fish perhaps, but hazardous to riverboats and rafts and fishers. Hazardous to the local economy too.

Maybe she'd made a mistake in stopping by the burnt acreage before heading up to the old farmhouse, but curiosity had gotten the best of her. According to her sister, Addie, who'd been helping their grandmother manage the farm since their dad died, only part of their land had been damaged by last year's wildfire. But from this vantage point, it looked far worse than Madison had imagined.

She looked east to where the Thompsons' neighboring hazelnut farm was—unrecognizable. Addie had told her how the Thompsons were burnt "clean" and how nothing, including their home and outbuildings, had survived. Madison spied a lonely brick chimney over by the river and what looked like a large camping trailer next to it. Was that all that was left? The vastness of the fire's rampage was hard to absorb. She'd seen photos and videos while overseas, but nothing compared to seeing the place firsthand.

Her eyes stung with unshed tears that she blamed on the acrid air that hung heavy in the aftermath of the morning rain, but the lump in her throat belied her. How could one not react to so much loss and devastation? She marveled at how cool Addie had sounded when she'd written Madison the full report last year. But other than the fate of the Thompsons, she'd barely mentioned the state of the rest of the area. Madison still wasn't sure who had been hit and who had been spared. But she'd observed many victims on her drive up the highway this morning. It seemed the wildfire had played some cruel version of leapfrog all along the river. Some places were untouched while others held nothing but stumps and cinders. It made no sense.

She wondered how long it would take for everyone along the river to recover. Or would they? Hopefully the Thompsons had good insurance on their hazelnut farm. Apparently none of the McDowells' agricultural losses were covered. But compared to the Thompson farm, they'd been lucky. Or "blessed," as Grandma had said in her last letter to Madison. "God spared us for a reason," she'd written in a shaky hand last November. She'd passed away only two weeks after sending that letter. Madison had longed to come home for the memorial service, but her teaching semester in Mongolia had just begun and there was no one to replace her. Now the only McDowells remaining were Addie and Madison. Co-owners of the Christmas tree farm. Partnering with her "baby" sister would be interesting. Especially considering how

Addie had never held any interest in agriculture. Even as a child, Addie had preferred to stay in the house, her nose in a book, to romping and roaming the great outdoors like her tomboy big sister.

Madison strolled over to the riverbank, curious as to whether the old oak tree and rope swing had survived. On her way through the burned area, she noticed a few spots of foliage near a large, charred stump. There in the midst of the defiant green plant bloomed bright orange daisy-like blossoms. Defiantly optimistic, as if to say, "There's still life here." She bent down to pick a flower. Studying its dark center, she remembered how Grandma had called these Mule's Ears. Madison smiled as she spied a number of these brave plants here and there, thriving in the darkened soil. But the old oak tree, though still standing, was blackened on one side, with no signs of life above. But perhaps its leaves had already fallen. And the old swing was nowhere to be seen.

She walked to the river's edge and peered below at the deep pool where the local kids used to swing out and jump—the perfect way to cool off on a hot summer day. Summers on the Christmas tree farm had been amazing. Even when Dad put her to work, it had been fun. And playtime always followed. She'd wanted those summers to go on forever, but it all would end right before Labor Day each year. Mom would drive from the city, pick her girls up, and take them back to their stuffy condo and nearby school.

That's how the joint custody agreement had been written. Madison would mope in her room for a few weeks, literally counting the days until she and Addie could return to the farm to spend Thanksgiving and Christmas with Dad and their grandparents. She envied local river kids like the Thompsons' brood whose parents were not divorced. Kids who got to live here in paradise year-round.

As she returned to her Jeep, she picked a few more Mule's

Ear flowers, making a small bouquet that she planned to give to Addie. She slid the stems into her water bottle, then smiled when she set it in the cupholder. Beauty from ashes . . . maybe there was hope after all. She started the engine and considered texting Addie that she was almost "home," but then decided it would be more fun to surprise her sister. Addie was such a meticulous planner, a real type A—maybe *triple A*—that it was fun to catch her off guard sometimes. Fun for Madison, anyway. Addie probably wouldn't appreciate it.

She drove slowly down the long, graveled driveway, beyond the burned area, and into the lush green rows of various-sized Douglas fir and spruce and noble fir trees. They were untouched by the fire, and she couldn't help but be amazed at the contrast. It was as if someone had simply drawn an invisible fire line, and the flames had stopped. Yet she knew that hadn't happened. Addie had already explained that the wind had just changed its course—in the nick of time—and leaped across the river instead of consuming the remainder of the farm. Whether it was the result of fickle wind or God, as Grandma claimed, it did seem slightly miraculous.

As the driveway curved, Madison spied the old red barn behind a protective grove of enormous fir trees that had been planted around seventy-five years ago, back when the barn was built. It was reassuringly intact. Perhaps in need of some fresh paint, but stalwartly standing with a somewhat wizened expression. What a wild scene it must've witnessed. Not far from the barn stood the old white farmhouse. Even from this distance, she could see it, too, needed fresh paint, and some of the shutters looked askew. But the old two-story remained brave and tall, as if to proclaim, "I'm a survivor."

She knew she should be encouraged by this section of the family farm. It really was a blessing that it was unscathed by the wind-driven blaze that had roared through here last summer. And yet her heart still felt heavy. So much loss . . . so much to be sorted out . . . so much work left to be done. In a way, like her own life. She'd been through her own wildfire of sorts . . . with Trevor. But that was safely behind her now. Something to be grateful for. Something to forget.

Being back here on the farm felt like a much-needed fresh start. Hopefully her baby sister would see it that way too.

Madison parked her Jeep in front of the wide front porch. The old wicker rockers were still there, and for a moment she imagined she saw Grandma out there, rising from a rocker with a huge smile and big wave to welcome her. Madison had always gotten along well with her grandmother. Perhaps because Madison's temperament was similar to Grandpa's. Both were fun-loving and adventurous risk-takers. Addie, who was more like their grandma, was dependable and responsible and reliable. But unlike Grandma, Addie could be a real stick-in-the-mud at times.

Still, Madison had to give her sister credit for stepping in to help after their dad got sick while Madison was out of the country. Madison had offered to stick around and help when she'd returned for Dad's funeral, but Addie had held her at arm's length, assuring her that everything was under "perfect control." In other words, Madison was not needed. And so Madison had returned to Mongolia to finish out her five-year commitment to teach English in a rural area. The fulfillment of a dream she'd nurtured during her tenure of teaching language arts in a Portland high school that was known for its high teacher turnover. But when her term of service had ended last spring, Madison had been eager to come back with hopes of being useful on the tree farm.

But once again, Addie insisted she didn't need any help. And so Madison had taken the opportunity to see more of the world on her way home. It seemed a good way to get Trevor out of her system. Traveling through Asia and Europe proved a good distraction to a broken heart. If she could call it that. The more time and space she put between her and Trevor, the more she realized it was probably a case of wounded pride and disappointment.

She got out of her Jeep and, with her wildflower bouquet in hand, went up the front porch steps. Just like the last time she'd been here, the boards as well as the handrail seemed a bit rickety. Worried about their elderly grandmother, Madison had mentioned this to Addie a time or two in emails. Addie had assured her she would get them fixed. Maybe she'd been too busy.

Madison peeked through the window of the old door, curious whether Addie was inside the house or working in the office next to the barn. She quietly knocked. Bracing herself for whatever kind of reception she was about to receive, she waited. When Addie didn't come, Madison let herself in. She felt a bit intrusive, but then she reminded herself she owned half of this farm and had every right to be here. Still, she wondered . . . how would Addie react? Oh, she knew that Madison was coming for a visit . . . eventually . . . But she probably didn't expect her sister today, or for her to stay on indefinitely.

The sound of footsteps on the pine plank floors came from the kitchen. Madison stood up straighter, waiting for what she hoped would be a happy reunion. But when Addie rounded the corner, her eyes opened wide, and she stopped so abruptly that her coffee sloshed onto her crisp white shirt.

"Madison!" she exclaimed. "What're you doing here?"

Madison's grin felt apologetic "Just happened to be in the neighborhood," she joked. But when Addie neither smiled nor laughed, Madison shrugged apologetically and held out her wildflower bouquet. "I thought it was time to come home."

"*Home?*" Addie pulled a neatly folded tissue from her pants pocket, then took her time to blot her soiled shirt before she looked up with slightly narrowed eyes. "You honestly think of the farm as your *home?*"

Madison didn't know what to say. Tilting her head to one side, she studied her younger sister. She was still as petite and pretty as always in that blue-eyed-blond, rosy-cheeked sort of way. So much like their mother. But Addie also had a new hardness about her that felt foreign to Madison. One thing hadn't changed however. Her baby sister hated surprises as much as ever.

2

Madison set her water bottle and flower arrangement on the old oak kitchen table and, pausing to look around, gathered her thoughts. The kitchen looked different than what she recalled from the last time she was here. Grandma's charming bric-a-brac and homey touches were sadly absent, and several shiny stainless kitchen appliances looked slightly out of place with the old painted cabinets. But at least they were still the same celery green. A little chipped perhaps, but the pale shade was familiar and comforting. Madison braced herself, slowly turning to see Addie carefully studying her.

"I've considered this farm home for as long as I can remember," Madison said evenly. "The whole time I've been out of the country, whenever I longed for home, it was always right here." She ran a hand over the old, stained butcher-block counter, remembering how many times she'd found fresh-baked cookies spread out here to cool. Gingersnaps had been her grandma's specialty.

"No offense, Madison, but I thought *the world was your home*." Addie refilled her coffee mug from another sleek appliance. "Wasn't it your plan to globe-trot forever? To teach English overseas with Trevor and—"

"Plans change," Madison said abruptly. "Trevor and I are history. And I've had enough of seeing the world."

"So the proverbial prodigal has returned." Addie watched Madison over the rim of her coffee mug as she took a long sip. "I'm sorry I forgot to kill the fatted calf."

Madison bristled but nodded toward the coffee maker. "Mind if I help myself?"

"Of course not. Mi casa es su casa." Addie's tone sounded cynical as she retrieved a white mug from the cabinet and handed it to her sister. "Make yourself at home."

As Madison filled the mug, she wondered what had become of Grandma's collection of funky, chipped mugs, most of them Christmassy and no two the same. "Things seem to have changed around here."

"Oh, not really." Addie leaned against the counter. "I mean, sure, I did a few upgrades after Grandma passed. I'd like to do a few more, but finances are tight."

"Really? What happened to Grandma's life insurance policy? She always used to tell me how that would help out after she was gone."

"Yes. It did help with funeral expenses," Addie snapped. "What little is left is safe in the bank. Not as much as you expected. And with taxes due . . ."

"That's okay . . . I didn't really expect anything." Madison frowned. "What's going on with you, Addie? You seem different. It's like you're angry at me for something."

"Angry?" Addie's pale brows arched. "No, I'm not angry." She let out a long sigh. "I guess I'm just tired. You know I've been carrying the load alone for a while now. Even more so since the fire."

"I know, and I appreciate it. But you must have some workers to help out."

Addie's laugh sounded sarcastic. "Are you kidding?"

She shrugged. "Grandma and Dad always had a few hired hands."

"Welcome to post-COVID, Madison. I don't know what it was like in Mongolia. But here in the US of A, the jobs are plentiful, but the workers are few."

"Then I guess it's good I came home. I always loved working here."

"Right." Addie did not sound convinced, and Madison had no clue how to smooth the rough waters between them. She peered into her sister's eyes, wishing she could see inside to whatever was eating her.

"How are *you*?" Madison asked. "I mean, *really*. Are you okay, Addie? Is something wrong? Is it because I didn't tell you I was coming home today? I'm sorry that I caught you off guard like this. I was hoping it'd be a good surprise. But I realize now you don't really like—"

"Oh, I'm sorry, Madison." Addie set down her coffee mug and opened her arms. "Welcome home, sis." For a long moment they embraced and, since they'd never been particularly huggy growing up, Madison hoped that meant things were okay now. After all, weren't sisters supposed to love and support each other?

"I've really missed you," Madison said as they stepped apart. "I meant to write more, Addie. But to be honest, there wasn't all that much to write about."

"Seriously? You're living on the other side of the world and there's nothing to write about?"

"You'd be surprised how mundane it was most of the time. Same old routine day in and day out." She sighed, then sipped her coffee. "And things with Trevor . . . well, like I said, that's over and done."

"I'm sorry. Maybe it was for the best?" Addie tipped her head to one side. "You wanna talk about it?"

Madison really did *not* want to talk about it. She wanted to forget about it. But worried saying so would hurt Addie's feelings, and longing for a genuine sisterly moment, she decided to give her the bare bones. "It's kind of cliché, really. Trevor and I hadn't been getting along that great. We had some disagreements about how the school was being run. Some power struggles since the culture respects male opinions whether or not their experiences back them up . . ."

Addie nodded, as if she understood.

"But in hindsight, it might've been something more . . ."

Addie's eyes sparked with interest. "What was that?"

"Well, a new teacher came last year. Isobel Porter from Savannah. Young and pretty and full of starry-eyed enthusiasm to be '*servin' on the mission field*.'" Madison faked Isobel's sugary southern accent perfectly. "And Isobel thought Trevor was the greatest thing since sliced bread." Madison grimaced to be caught using one of Grandpa's favorite catchphrases.

"Wow, not so different from my story with Boyd," Addie said. "Guess you should be thankful you weren't married like I was. Keeps breaking up simpler."

"I guess." Madison shrugged. She preferred to forget how often Trevor had strung her along—at well-chosen moments—with sweet insinuations that they'd soon be married . . . but never actually saying the words she'd longed to hear. She should've known better. But when she and Trevor first met, while teaching in the same high school in Portland, they'd had similar dreams. And attending the mission conference together, they'd seemed so in sync, so meant to be, too good to be true. And it had been.

"Well, I'm sorry you got hurt." Addie put a hand on her shoulder. "And I'm sorry I wasn't more welcoming. It's hard to admit it, but I guess I've been a little overwhelmed."

"Which is precisely why I'm here to help."

Addie just nodded.

"I stopped by the burn area," Madison said solemnly.

"Sad, huh?"

"Yeah. Any plans? Fall's the perfect time to replant."

"Sure, if you have workers. But don't forget, it's also time to trim trees, make wreaths, take orders, and get the place ready for the holidays. Just thinking of all that makes me super tired this year. I mean, last year was bad enough. Everything came to a screeching halt here when Grandma passed."

"Well, you've got me here to help you now." Madison slipped

an arm around Addie's shoulders in big-sister fashion. "Somehow we'll get 'er done."

Addie didn't look too sure, and her smile looked forced. "I was just heading to the office. Have bookwork to do. Deferred taxes and things to catch up on."

"While you're doing that, I'll get settled and unpack. Then if you don't mind, I'll poke around the property some. I want to get acclimated and see what needs doing." She smiled bravely. "I'm ready to roll up my sleeves." Madison pointed to the fridge. "But I'm kind of hungry. Mind if I—"

"No, of course not. Help yourself to anything. I'm a little low on groceries, but like I said, mi casa es su casa, only I mean it this time."

"Maybe I can make a store run later." She frowned. "Is Riverside Market still there or did it burn?"

"Amazingly, it survived. Storefronts burned out on both sides, but the little store's okay. Although Jack sold it, and it's not as well stocked anymore. It's called Borden's Market now. They make up for lack of inventory with higher prices." Addie wrinkled her nose. "Makes it worth driving to town. Well, depending on gas prices." Addie pointed out the kitchen window to where Madison's little, red Jeep Wrangler was parked in front. "Is that yours or a rental you'll need to return?"

"It's all mine. Well, the bank and me. I saved enough in Mongolia for a good-size down payment. Thought having my own wheels might come in handy here."

"And you probably get better gas mileage than Grandpa's old flatbed. That's what I was going to suggest you drive." Addie reached for a coat hanging by the door. "You know where I am if you need me."

Madison waved goodbye, then refilled her coffee mug. Even though she was relieved to have the old farmhouse to herself and to have patched things up, sort of, with Addie, she still felt uneasy. Or maybe she felt unsettled. Or just plain discombobulated. She knew she'd experienced culture shock after five years in rural Mongolia, but now she felt like she was having a different kind of experience. It was more than just adjusting to changes, and there had been plenty. She felt like this was about loss.

She walked through the living room and was somewhat consoled to see that little had changed in here. Addie had removed a lot of the doodads and clutter, but that was probably an improvement. Less things to collect dust. Grandpa's old La-Z-Boy recliner was in the same spot next to the front picture window, where he could spy on anyone coming up the driveway. A good location at Christmastime when someone would inevitably show up right after he'd sat down with his newspaper and pipe. But he'd pop up, with pipe in hand, grab his wool coat, and hurry out to help them find the perfect tree.

"Word-of-mouth advertising is what keeps us in business," he'd remind anyone who questioned his devotion to his customers. "As soon as McDowell's Family Christmas Tree Farm runs out of Christmas spirit, we'll be out of business."

Madison sat down on Grandma's burgundy velvet rocker-recliner, fingering the edge of an old granny square afghan that Grandma crocheted. One of many. Madison had one of her own stored in a trunk up in her room. But this afghan was special because it was all in Christmas colors. Grandma had always felt their home needed to reflect Christmas. Her Christmas pillows, as always, lined the sagging green velvet sofa on the opposite wall. Although it looked as if Addie had thinned the herd since there was now room to sit. And above the big stone fireplace, the painting of a Christmassy winter scene still proudly hung, and the mantel held a selection of red and green candles.

The room was a bit out of fashion but charmingly cozy. Especially when there was a fire crackling. It looked just like a Christmas scene you'd see on a greeting card. Here and there were antiques Grandma had collected from friends and family and garage sales over time, and the old braided rug, in its faded shades of red and green, anchored the pieces together. In its own way, the room was perfect.

Madison gazed out the window. Beyond the driveway, she could see past the tall fir trees to where the Thompsons' grove of hazelnut trees once thrived. Now there was just blackened soil. And beyond that, the lonely chimney. She wondered about the camp trailer. Did someone live there? Mr. and Mrs. Thompson had to be in their seventies by now. Maybe one of their six kids? Or maybe grandkids? The older Thompson kids would probably be close to fifty by now. Although Gavin and Mindy, the babies of the family, were closer to her age.

Over the years she'd learned not to think of Gavin . . . much. It seemed that, by now, well over twenty years later, she'd have forgotten her first crush. But sometimes, to her angst, the memories still stung. Last she'd heard, Gavin was happily married with two kids—one that was probably college age and the other much younger. Well, good for him!

3

Madison took her time getting settled into her old bedroom. To her relief, nothing had changed in here. Judging by the dust and musty smell, no one had even been in the garret room since her last visit. She opened the window to let in the fresh autumn air. It was late September, but the day was warming up to feel like summer. She dusted and cleaned and laundered the linens from her room and then, just like Grandma used to do, she hung them on the line outside. Grandma's clothesline went right over her hedge of lavender, which still had blooms. What a treat to have lavender-scented, sunshine-dried sheets! As she hung the last pillowcase, she remembered the time she'd strung up a clothesline outside the women's dorm in Mongolia only to discover everything missing by the time she went to bring her laundry inside. Fortunately, she assumed, that would not happen here.

As she set the laundry basket on the front porch, she heard the sound of some kind of engine growling nearby. Peering in the direction of the sound, she observed a long, dark trail of sooty dust following what looked like a motorized minibike riding along the border of the Thompsons' land. Curious about this and concerned that the ashy cloud would soil her nice clean linens, she decided to investigate its source. But by the time she reached the trail the bike was creating, the rider was clear on the other side of the property.

"Time to meet our neighbors," she said to herself as she strolled over to the camp trailer. Glad she still had on her boots since the sooty dust was everywhere, she quietly knocked on the trailer's door, feeling slightly intrusive. When no one answered, she knocked harder.

"Can I help you?" A male voice behind her made her jump.

"Oh." She turned quickly to see a man with dark hair, slightly tinged with gray, and a neatly trimmed beard strolling toward her. He stopped in his tracks at the sight of her, his dark eyes widening in surprise.

"Madison?" He peered curiously at her. "Madison McDowell?"

"Yes." She nodded nervously, studying him. "Do I know you?"

"You used to. I'm Gavin. Gavin Thompson." He chuckled as he rubbed his beard. "I suppose I've changed. I discovered a beard is pretty low maintenance when living in a trailer."

"You live here?" She resisted the urge to visibly gulp. This was really Gavin? The boy she remembered from her teen years?

"Yep." He nodded, continuing forward with his hand outstretched. She extended her hand, which he firmly grasped and then, to her surprise, used to pull her into a friendly embrace. "It's so good to see you, Madison."

"Yes." She stepped back, smoothing her denim jacket with a stiff smile on her face as she tried to keep her pounding heart from giving her away. "Good to see you too, Gavin."

He shoved his hands into his jeans pockets. "So you must be back from China. Your grandmother told me about your teaching job there. Sounds exciting." He grinned. "You always were such an adventurous gal."

"To be honest, it wasn't as exciting as some might think. But it was certainly different. And the country and the people were absolutely amazing." She folded her arms in front of her. "But, seriously, you thought I was adventurous?"

"Sure. You're the only girl I knew who was brave enough to jump off the railroad bridge."

She looked into his midnight-blue eyes, remembering how they'd always reminded her of the deepest pools in the river. Cool and dark, but she didn't want to drown in them, or get pulled down by an unseen eddy. "So you, uh, you're staying here full-time? Not just camping?"

"That's right." He patted the side of the trailer. "My current abode. Well, me and Lily."

"Your wife?" For some reason she didn't remember his wife's name, but she didn't think it was Lily.

"No. Lily's my daughter. The younger one. Lucy is in college. Her last year too, I hope."

"Oh, right." She wanted to ask where his wife was but couldn't string the words together. "You don't seem old enough to have a daughter in her last year of college."

"Well, you might recall that Shelby and I got an early start."

She felt her cheeks warming. Of course, her name was Shelby. How could she forget that? It all flooded back to her now . . . how Gavin had married Shelby Fraley straight out of high school! Madison also remembered how she, at sixteen, had been dumb-founded to show up for summer on the tree farm to learn that her teenage crush was married! Who got married at eighteen? When Gavin and Shelby's first child came along before the next Christmas, she had her answer. But no one knew how deeply she'd been hurt by what felt like a total betrayal, or how long it took her to get over it.

"Well, I didn't mean to intrude," she said in an uneasy tone. "I was actually just curious about that kid on the dirt bike."

"That kid is Lily. She won't even be twelve until January, but she's already a serious dirt biker. Competes and everything."

"Interesting." Madison looked out to where the dirt bike rider, as if on cue, suddenly came roaring up from behind the pickup. Hopping off in a cloud of dark dust, the slender girl tugged off her bright blue helmet to shake loose a head of curly auburn hair that reminded Madison of Shelby. She set her helmet on her bike seat and looked curiously at Madison.

"Lily, I want you to meet our neighbor, Madison McDowell."

"McDowell like the Christmas tree farm?"

"That's right." Madison smiled.

Lily cocked her head to one side. "I already met Addie, but I didn't know she had a roommate." She wiped soot from her hands onto the front of her soot-covered jeans, although it didn't seem to help.

"I'm Addie's sister," Madison explained. "I haven't been able to visit here for the last five years."

"Madison's been in China," Gavin told Lily.

"Mongolia, actually." Madison nodded toward Lily's bike. "I hear you're pretty good on that thing."

Lily shrugged. "I'm okay."

"I was wondering, uh, would you mind not riding so close to our property line?"

Lily's brows drew together. "Why?"

"Oh, well, it stirs up the dust, you know . . . and the noise."

Lily looked at Gavin. "*Daaad?*"

"Madison makes a good point," Gavin told his daughter. "We need to be good neighbors."

"But what about the trail we're building?" she said in protest. "It *has* to go along the border. Like we drew it in our plans."

"Trail?" Madison asked. "Plans?"

"Lily's been dreaming of turning this place into a dirt bike park. You know, a destination place for other young riders like her to come and attend training workshops, camp with their families, and maybe even hold competitions."

"Seriously? Here?"

"Yeah," Lily said sharply. "Why not?"

"Well, this has always been an agricultural area," Madison said lamely. "I mean, there might be some kind of zoning restrictions."

Gavin laughed. "No worries. There are no restrictions like that out here. I already checked."

"But what about your hazelnut orchards? Don't you plan to replant them?" Madison looked out over the blackened, barren land. "You can't just leave it like *this*."

"Of course, I'll plant some trees for shade and greenery. Maybe some grassy areas around the house and the cabins. But I have no desire to be a filbert farmer."

"Me neither," Lily chimed in with a defiant tone. "And Dad promised me a dirt bike course here. That's why we sold our house and moved out here in the first place. We already mapped it all out with trails and camping areas and everything."

"What about the rest of your family?" Madison asked Gavin. "Do your parents and siblings think this is a good idea?"

"My dad passed on and Mom's in memory-care assisted living. My brothers and sisters were glad to sell their shares of the property to me after the fire took everything."

"Oh." Madison couldn't imagine the negative impact a noisy dirt bike park would have on their Christmas tree farm. The whole thing felt haphazard and totally inappropriate to the quiet agricultural area. She wanted to ask if his wife approved but knew that might come out wrong too. She'd already stepped on Lily's toes. "Well, I don't really know what to say about all this. It's a lot to take in. I'm curious what other neighbors along the river will think."

"Most people are still figuring out how to rebuild their own properties," Gavin told her. "They weren't all as fortunate as you and Addie with your tree farm."

"Yes, I know. I realize these are hard times for everyone. I just don't see how a noisy dirt bike park will make anything better."

Lily stepped forward with both hands on her hips and stared defiantly into Madison's eyes. "This is gonna be a really cool place for kids and families to come. You'll see. There'll be hills and dips and all sorts of cool stuff. It's gonna be awesome, so you might as well get used to it."

"Lily," Gavin scolded. "Show some respect."

The girl stepped back. "Sorry, Dad." She reached for her helmet, then shoved it back onto her head.

"Well, it was nice to meet you, Lily." Madison forced a smile. "I'm sure we can think of some ways to make everyone happy about this. Maybe some sort of compromise?"

"I have riding to do," Lily said as she slung a leg over her bike.

"Yes. And I should go too." Madison slowly backed away from Gavin. "Good to see you. And sorry to have troubled you." As the dirt bike roared to life, Madison hurried toward home. What a mess. And unless she was mistaken, it would probably get messier.

4

Madison stormed into the house. In the short walk back from her "visit" with the neighbors, she'd had time to get even more irritated. It was fine for Gavin to want to create a motorbike park for his daughter, but had he considered how it might affect his farming neighbors? The noise, the dust, the traffic? This had always been such a quiet, bucolic stretch on the river. Sure, things had changed since the fire, but was that any reason to introduce an enterprise like a bike park?

Madison wondered what Gavin's wife thought about this wild development. Shelby had always seemed like such a girlie girl to Madison. She remembered how Shelby would act too scared to jump from the rope swing. Or how she'd cry for help, insisting she needed one of the guys to grab the swing for her, or to help her get off lest she fall and break a nail. And she always needed help climbing down the steep, rocky riverbank to get into the water. Naturally she'd be wearing some impractical, bejeweled flip-flops. Then she'd complain about how scary the current was, even if it was barely moving. Or how cold the river was. She'd sit shivering onshore in her skimpy bikini as if she was suffering with hypothermia. What Gavin ever saw in Shelby Fraley had totally baffled Madison. Well, besides her looks. But Madison just couldn't imagine Shelby approving of her disheveled daughter and her dirt bike dreams.

Back in the house, she surveyed the kitchen for groceries. Addie hadn't been kidding. The fridge and cabinets were sadly barren. Other than some rice cakes, a couple of yogurts, and some wilted lettuce, it was slim pickings around here. Judging by the trash, Addie dined mostly on takeout. Perhaps her baby sister would appreciate a home-cooked meal for a change. Not wanting to disturb Addie in her office, where a letter from Grandma had mentioned Addie spent most of her time, Madison left a note and headed to the closest grocery store.

Although her sister had complained about limited selection and high prices in Borden's Market, Madison thought it still seemed way better stocked than what had been available in Mongolia. Americans just didn't understand how good they had it! As she loaded a basket with produce, she ran into some old acquaintances and asked how they'd fared in the fire. Marsha Procter described how they were already rebuilding their barn. The Graydon farm, like the McDowells', had escaped unscathed. Madison was tempted to ask what they thought about having a noisy, dusty dirt bike park nearby, but she suspected that, with it not being near their land, they might not even care. And maybe she was silly to care. Maybe her problem wasn't really the tree farm's proximity to the dirt bike park . . . but to Gavin.

"You're new 'round here," the cashier said as he rang up her groceries. He appeared to be about her age and wasn't bad looking. He had a nice smile too.

"Not exactly new." She introduced herself, making sure to mention the tree farm.

"Oh, yeah. So you must be related to Addie." He put her lettuce into the bag.

"My sister."

"Well, I'm Jeb Borden." He shook her hand. "Nice to meet you."

"Borden? Do you own this store?"

"Yep. Well, me and the bank."

"You're lucky it survived the fire."

"I'll say. I only bought it from the Campbells two years ago." He waved a hand toward the new coffee bar. "I did all these upgrades and changed a few things right before the fire." He grimly shook his head. "Then while we were evacuated over in the valley, I was literally biting my nails, assuming it'd all gone up in smoke."

"I imagine business has been a little slow for you."

"Summer was pretty disappointing. No tourists. But the locals are supportive."

"Hopefully things will start picking up soon."

He nodded. "The Christmas season might help with folks coming up here for trees. Will you folks be doing U-cut this year?"

"I don't see why not. People still like to cut their own trees, don't they?"

"Oh, sure. At least I think they do. I just meant since you didn't do it last year." He scanned her last item, then told her the total. She handed him her bank card. "We didn't?"

"Nope. Addie said it was too much work with no employees." Madison considered this as she waited for her card to process. "I've heard it's hard getting workers since COVID, but my grandpa used to entice high schoolers out to the farm. They always seemed to enjoy it."

Jeb shrugged. "I've hired teenagers too. Now I don't need them so much." He returned her card. "Speaking of kids, what d'ya think of that new dirt bike park going in next to you? That ought to bring in some tourist traffic by next spring. I've already been telling my friends who've got kids about it. Such a great idea. Can't wait to see it up and running."

Madison just nodded as he handed her the receipt.

"Nice to meet ya, Madison." Jeb flashed a wide smile. "Tell that sister of yours *hey* for me. And tell her not to be such a stranger." He winked as if he wanted her to get his meaning. He was obviously into Addie. And why not, she was a real cutie-pie.

But for some reason, her sister wasn't a fan of this market. Was it because of Jeb?

· · ·

It was late afternoon by the time Madison got home. As she took her sheets off the clothesline, the sun dipped below the tree-tops and the air cooled. To her relief, her linens were soot-free and fresh smelling. Maybe she had overreacted about the dirt bike park. Maybe it was a good idea. She just needed to get used to it.

She was just going up the porch steps when she heard a motor loudly revving. She looked over to see Lily zipping past in a familiar cloud of dark dust. The bike was so close to the boundary line that Madison suspected she'd actually strayed onto McDowell property. Was Lily trying to make a point?

Maybe it was time to put up a fence. Or a living hedge of Christmas trees. That might help keep the dust out, but it would be impossible to keep the noise out. She hated to imagine how loud it might get with a whole bunch of kids zipping around and around over there. Seriously, what was Gavin thinking? Did that man let his children rule him? Shaking her head, she went inside, quickly closing the door against the intrusive noise.

"There you are," Addie called as she came down the hallway. "I smelled something good in the kitchen, but you'd disappeared."

She hefted her laundry basket onto her hip. "Getting my laundry off the line."

"My, my . . . aren't we domestic?"

"I just wanted to freshen up my room." Madison set the basket at the foot of the stairs. "It's kind of musty up there."

"Well, if you'd given me more notice, I might've had a chance to—"

"I didn't want you to lift a finger on my behalf."

"You probably just remember my housekeeping skills, or lack of . . ."

"Well, you just have different interests," Madison said lightly.

Addie glanced toward the kitchen. "So what's cooking in there?"

"Spaghetti with meat sauce."

"Meat sauce?" Addie frowned. "I'm a vegetarian."

Madison suppressed the urge to roll her eyes as she headed for the kitchen.

"Did you already mix them together?"

"Not yet." Madison stirred the pasta pot. "The sauce is simmering while the pasta cooks." She pulled out a string of spaghetti and bit into it. "Almost done too."

"I'll just have my pasta with butter."

"I got some good parmesan you could put on top." Madison opened the fridge. "Unless you're off dairy too."

"No, that was just too ambitious for me."

Madison pulled out a head of lettuce. "Wanna help me make a salad?"

"Sure. Let me wash off the office grit first."

As they chopped veggies for a salad, Madison brought up the subject of the Thompsons' plans for next door.

"Oh, yeah, I know all about that." Addie's tone was nonchalant.

"You're not concerned? I mean, about the noise and the dust?" Madison knew Addie well enough to suspect she'd find something like this irritating.

"Oh, we'll get used to it. No big deal."

Madison stared at her sister. "Seriously? You don't care that it will change the whole feel of this farm? I mean, it's always been such a quiet, peaceful place. Doesn't it bother you to imagine a bunch of kids yelling and screaming and squirreling around on noisy bikes? And the dust? What about that?"

Addie shrugged as she slid chopped cucumbers into the salad bowl. "I think you're overblowing it. It won't be as bad as all that."

Madison was flabbergasted. What had become of her persnickety baby sister, the type A girl who didn't like to get her hands dirty? "I'm not so sure, Addie. I think it's a mess just waiting to happen. I honestly don't understand why Gavin is giving in to

Lily on this crazy whim of hers. Good grief, she's only eleven and it sounds like she rules the roost. And what does Shelby think? She was always such a—"

Addie's eyes grew wide. "Don't you know?"

"Know what?"

"Shelby died."

Madison set down her knife on the chopping block with a clunk. "She died?"

"Yeah. A couple years ago."

Madison was speechless. And stunned . . . she even felt guilty, as if she'd been speaking ill of the dead. Something Grandma used to warn about. Not that Madison had voiced an opinion on Shelby. Or had she? She knew she'd judged the woman in her mind. Maybe for years. "I had no idea. How did she die?"

Addie reached for a green pepper. "Car wreck."

Madison tried to remember if she'd said anything even slightly derogatory to Gavin about his wife. She didn't think so. She suddenly felt ashamed how her opinions had been spawned by teenage jealousy. She had hardly even known the woman. "Oh . . . that's so sad. Poor Gavin."

"And the girls, losing their mother." Addie shook her head. "It's been especially hard on Lily. I think she's the main reason Gavin decided to move back here. Well, that and the fire. His brothers and sisters wanted no part of the filbert business after all the trees were gone. No one wanted to replant."

"Yeah, he mentioned he'd bought them out."

Addie chopped the stem from the pepper. "And since he doesn't need the money, he can pretty much do what he wants with the property. And Lily clearly wants a dirt bike park. She got into dirt bikes after Shelby died. Gavin said it really brought her back to life. Before that she wasn't interested in anything. She got into scrapes with other kids, and her grades slipped. Their deal is she gets to ride dirt bikes as long as she gets along with her peers and keeps her grades up. Apparently it's done the trick too."

"Wow, sounds like you've really gotten to know their situation."

"Just trying to be a good neighbor." Addie's grin looked slightly sly. "And maybe something more too."

Madison felt her eyebrows arching. "Something more?"

"Well, Gavin's a great guy. Not bad looking and well-set financially. He'd be a pretty nice catch." She started to peel a carrot. "And Lily really needs a good influence. She's gotten so scruffy that Gavin's concerned. I've tried to help out as much as I can. I've had her overnight here a few times. Their trailer's shower is so tiny. I get her to take a proper bath and do something with that wild head of hair. Man, you should see the ring on the bathtub after she's done. And those fingernails! They get so black with soot, I wonder if they'll ever come clean."

Madison remembered Lily wiping her hands on her jeans. "That's really sweet that you're helping her, Addie."

"That's what neighbors do." Addie rinsed off her knife, then looked around the kitchen. "If I'd known you were fixing such a nice dinner, I would've invited them to join us. I'm not much of a cook, but I've had them over a few times. They really seem to appreciate it."

"It's probably a challenge cooking in that trailer."

"Yeah. They do a lot of outdoor stuff. Usually burgers on the grill. They've had me over there too a few times. It's like camping."

"You used to hate camping."

"Well, people can change. It's kinda cool to sit around the firepit and look at the stars. We've even made s'mores."

"Sounds fun." Madison could hear the flat tone of her voice as she drained the steaming pasta into a colander. It sounded like Addie was really endearing herself to Gavin and Lily.

"Are you okay?" Addie asked with concern in her eyes.

"Oh, sure. Maybe a little tired. It was a long drive down here from Seattle. I've been up since four this morning." And, sure, she was a little weary . . . but that wasn't what was troubling her.

After pretending to enjoy dinner while Addie chirped on and

on about how great things were between her and Gavin and Lily—like one happy family—Madison excused herself to her room. Despite her lavender-scented sheets and comfy bed, she wasn't the least bit tired, and the evening breeze suddenly felt cold to her. Everything felt cold to her, and she wondered what she was even doing here. Had she come back just in time to witness Addie and Gavin embarking on a romance? She didn't think her heart could possibly take that kind of hurt again.

5

Madison got out of bed to close her window and then paused there to look out. From this vantage point, she could easily see Gavin's camp trailer. Rather, the golden lights from the trailer since it was dark. It was actually a cozy scene with what looked like a dying-down campfire not far from the trailer. And was that Gavin bending over it, giving it a poke? Bright orange sparks shot up into the night sky, making the scene even more picturesque. She sighed with longing.

Gavin was a widower.

She shivered in the darkness. Barefoot in her old cotton nightgown, she stared blankly out the window. When her thoughts started to wander, retracing a bittersweet trail she rarely allowed herself to travel, she didn't try to stop them. She was transported back to that last magical summer with Gavin. A season that haunted her still.

June began brightly, like any other highly anticipated summer vacation on the tree farm. Being warmly welcomed, settling into her own room, helping Grandma with inside tasks, or driving the tractor, fixing the drip lines, and working outside with Dad and Grandpa. Wonderful, blissful routines.

As usual, when it was hot and the chores were done, she'd meet up with the local kids down by the river. As always, Gavin and his younger sister, Mindy, were part of this crowd. Gavin was seventeen and more handsome than ever. About to start his senior year, he brimmed with confidence and energy and enthusiasm. Madison and Mindy were only fifteen, but with a full year of high school behind them, they felt much older.

Addie was eleven and often had her nose in a book. She was too young to be welcome with the teens, but she'd tag along sometimes anyway—until her complaints about feeling left behind got everyone fed up. Addie had been such a whiner back then. And like everyone else except Mindy, Addie had been oblivious to the budding romance between Gavin and Madison, including the fact that they wanted to ditch her at times.

Madison had always admired Gavin. And over the years, she'd often showed off for his benefit. She'd even feign false courage hoping to impress him. Of course, once she took the risk—like leaping from the railroad bridge—she usually got such a thrill that the next time was easy. But up until that last sweet summer, her relationship with Gavin had been similar to Mindy's. He'd been a big brother and good friend. But when Mindy started spending more time with Gavin's best buddy, Ben, it seemed a natural transition for Madison to become more involved with Gavin. Before summer ended, she was head over heels for him. Even now, the memory of their first kiss still sent her spinning.

But unlike Mindy, who'd loved sharing steamy stories about Ben, Madison had been determined to keep her relationship with Gavin limited. Although they had some pretty hot make-out sessions, she always knew when to draw the line. Gavin might not have appreciated it so much in the moment, but he always respected her for it. And that was nice.

Of course, their amazing summer ended far too soon. And on the last Friday before Labor Day, they met at their favorite rendezvous—the oak tree by the river—where Gavin used his flashlight to reveal the initials he'd carved into the gnarly old trunk. GT + MM. After a final memorable kissing session, Madison heard her dad's shrill whistle, the signal for her curfew. The young lovers kissed goodbye and swore to meet at Thanksgiving and to write letters in the meantime.

But Madison's mom spoiled their Thanksgiving "date" by insisting her girls accompany her to Spokane to meet her new fiancé's family—and to celebrate their engagement. And then, come Christmas break, Mom and Ray ruined everything by having the girls return to Spokane for holiday festivities and a New Year's Eve wedding.

Following winter break, the letters, which had already been scarce on Gavin's end, grew even scarcer. Knowing his senior year was demanding, Madison excused him for it, but still wrote his name on her notebook, daydreaming of their next meeting. By spring break, she was desperate to see him. But Gavin and Mindy were gone. They were off with their church youth group, building houses in Guadalajara, Mexico. As it turned out, Shelby went on that mission trip too.

By summer break it was too late. Gavin and Shelby were married! It was mind-blowing but true. And Madison's sixteenth summer was a dark one. Nobody knew why she was so moody. Grandma blamed it on teenage hormones, Dad blamed her newlywed "parents" back in Spokane, and preteen Addie, making the most of Madison's retreat into the shadows, basked in the limelight for a change.

Now, standing by the window, Madison closed the bedroom curtains and turned away, wiping tears from her cheeks that she hadn't even realized she'd cried. Gavin was available now. But once again, Madison was too late. Based on Addie's comments, it was painfully clear that her sister was staking out her territory. She was set on Gavin. And really, the match made sense. It had never occurred to Madison before, but Addie and Shelby were strikingly similar. Both were pretty, soft, needy . . . the kind of women that made a guy feel manly, strong . . . necessary. The way that Trevor had claimed he wanted to feel. Attributes, according to him, that Madison lacked.

6

By the next morning, Madison was determined to put her concerns over a potential romance between Addie and Gavin behind her. It was simply her tiredness that had taken over her emotions last night. She was stronger than that. In the light of day, she realized how much she loved the tree farm. And she wasn't about to allow anything to drive her out. Not that easily.

Over the next several days, she fell into a routine of sorts. Madison had learned to appreciate cooking in Mongolia, and having a "modern" kitchen back here in the States made it even more rewarding. She enjoyed fixing oatmeal, muffins, or whatever sounded good for breakfast.

Addie sometimes partook but usually preferred to take a yogurt and coffee to her office. There she would stay for most of the day, assuring Madison she could take care of her own lunch—"so please don't bother about me."

While Addie worked in the office, Madison poked around the farm, doing minor repairs and tending to neglected maintenance chores. She tried to ignore the noise next door and distracted herself from thinking about Gavin by keeping busy. After a few days, she began to explore the burn area further. The soil actually looked rich with nutrients left over from the fire, like it was just waiting to be replanted. She was curious about what it would take to start that process, but each time she raised the issue with Addie, she was shut down. Being the newcomer, she still felt slightly intrusive and decided to bide her time for a full week. But by the beginning of October, she could hold back no longer. While Addie filled a coffee mug, Madison broached the subject, determined to be firmer this time.

"We really need to start planting seedlings." Madison reached for the coffeepot to refill her own mug.

"I already told you, it's not in the budget."

"But it's an investment in our future, and if we start planting along the Thompsons' border, we can create a natural barrier between us and the motorbike park. It might not keep out much noise, but it could really help hold back the dust."

"Maybe so, but we can't do it now." Addie looked away. "We'd need to wait until spring."

"But fall is the perfect time to replant," Madison said.

"Fir trees can be planted any time of year," Addie called over her shoulder as she hurried for the door.

Madison trailed her. "But Dad and Grandpa always replanted in the fall. Fewer trees will die, and they have a better chance to get established. Plus, we don't have to irrigate until next summer, which saves on water."

"Maybe so, but we just can't afford it right now."

Madison blocked her sister from going down the porch steps. "I think *I* can afford it."

Addie's brows lifted. "You can afford to pay for trees and labor? On your own?"

"I still have some savings." Madison moved out of Addie's way. "I can afford to buy some seedlings. And if labor is too expense, I might just plant them myself."

Addie chuckled. "Well, feel free, sis. Knock yourself out."

That wasn't exactly the answer Madison had hoped for, but

maybe if Addie saw that she was serious, she would realize it was a smart business move after all. Then maybe, when they started filling their Christmas tree shipping orders, which had to be coming right up, the cash would start rolling in, and they could purchase more seedlings to plant.

Madison watched her sister head across the yard and over to her office, which was housed in a small cabinlike structure their dad had built years ago. She hadn't been inside in ages, but she remembered how it was always a mess of haphazard file cabinets and storage boxes and a mishmash of dusty junk. But it was also cool inside, and the pine walls were woodsy smelling. She was tempted to follow Addie over there and ask for help in how to place an order for tree plugs. That was what Dad had called the bundles that came in the fall—tree plugs. The planting always took place after the girls had gone back to school, but Madison had spent a gap year here at the farm before starting college. She'd thought maybe she wanted to be a tree farmer, but the work was harder than expected, and the farm life was pretty boring for an eighteen-year-old. Plus, it was painful seeing Gavin and Shelby and their baby when they visited his parents' filbert farm from time to time. By the next fall, she was glad to escape the whole scene and head off to college.

She sat on the porch and whipped out her phone to do a quick internet search of Douglas fir seedlings. Just how many trees would it take to plant an acre? To her surprise, tree plugs were surprisingly cheap. Even more so if purchased in bulk. But it could take up to fifteen hundred to fill an acre. And the burn area was probably close to five acres, give or take. That equaled a lot of trees! She did the math for four acres and grimaced. Six thousand trees sounded overwhelming, but she knew the soil in the burn area was pretty soft, so planting shouldn't be too hard. Especially if she could get some high schoolers to help on weekends and after school like her dad used to do. And so she decided to go for it.

When she called in her order, the woman on the other end hemmed and hawed and made it sound like it would be a long wait before the trees shipped. "Maybe by spring."

Not disguising her disappointment, Madison explained how they lived in the burn area and had really hoped to get to planting sooner than spring. "Just to keep down the dust, you know?"

"Well now, that might change things. We're committed to prioritizing the victims of the burn. No one wants to see good soil eroded during winter. Tell me your name and location, and I'll see what we can do."

"We're the McDowell's Family Christmas Tree Farm." She listed off the address.

"Oh, yeah. You're along the river, aren't you? That gives you a higher priority. Can you hold while I check on a few things?"

"Yes, of course." While Madison waited, she said a silent prayer, hoping this woman could do something.

"Good news," the woman finally announced. "We can get fir plugs to you as soon as within a week."

"Really?" Madison gulped, suddenly remembering how many trees she had asked for.

"My boss was surprised you hadn't placed an order sooner, but we just had a cancellation, so you're in luck."

Madison took a deep breath and, steadying herself, finished her order. Then, questioning her sensibilities, she sat down at the kitchen table. Had she lost it? Depleting her savings by ordering six thousand trees that would all arrive within a week? What was wrong with her?

She remembered what Jeb at the market had said about his difficulty finding workers. What if she couldn't get help? But didn't kids need money these days? If she offered this opportunity in Mongolia, kids would be lining up. She decided to go pay the local high school a visit. After all, she was an experienced high school teacher and had even toyed with the idea of substituting.

No time like the present to get to know whoever was in charge. Kill two birds with one stone.

The school allowed her to put up her Help Wanted poster and gave her information about certification for substituting. But as she got into her Jeep, she didn't feel very hopeful.

"Getting kids to work is like pulling teeth these days," the woman at the front desk had said lightly before Madison left. "Good luck, honey."

As she drove, Madison wondered how many trees one person could plant in one working day and how much one day would cost her at the hourly wage she was offering, just above minimum wage. She tried to do the math in her head as she drove to the farm but finally realized it wasn't that simple.

She knew that it would help to plant in soft ground, and it wasn't that hard to plant a tree plug. But how long would it actually take? She went to the tool shed and found a planting hoe and, although she had no plug to put in the ground, she went through the motions while counting the seconds.

Plunge the hoe into the soft ground to create a slit-like hole, push the small seedling in, then stomp the dirt down around it. She might've been optimistic, but it seemed fairly easily done within a minute or less. Of course, she still had to measure to the next hole, keep the line straight, and start over. And people were not machines. But planting fifty seedlings within an hour seemed reasonable to her.

She went into the house, got out a notepad, opened the calculator on her phone, and attempted to figure it out. She tried not to scold herself for not doing her homework first, but she'd always been the girl who jumped first and thought about it later. She finally calculated that fifteen hard workers, putting in an eight-hour shift, could probably get all the trees planted in a single day! Good news, but would she be able to find fifteen willing people? She also knew that if she kept them damp, the tree plugs could live for days outside of the ground, especially in this cool autumn air. Worst-case scenario, if she had no willing workers, it would take her a couple of weeks to plant them all herself. If it didn't kill her.

She was in pretty good shape, but performing hard labor for fifteen full workdays sounded like a challenge. Still, if she could get just one other worker, they could cut the time in half. And three would make thirds. With this in mind, she decided to pay a visit to the office. Besides everything else she needed to share with Addie, she was getting curious as to what could possibly keep her sister that busy for a full day every single day. No one else had ever spent that much time in the office before. Not only that, but Addie had been a bookkeeper, so she probably did most of her work electronically, which should be a real time-saver. Madison knocked gently on the door. And when there was no answer, she knocked louder.

It took a couple minutes before the door cracked open. "Oh, it's you," Addie said with a tinge of irritation in her tone. "What do you need?"

"I need to talk with you." Madison nudged the door. "Can I come in?"

"Well, I'm in the middle of—"

"It'll only take a minute." Madison shoved the door fully open to discover that the office looked nothing like it had before. The pine walls had been whitewashed, making the space appear brighter and cleaner, and the old file cabinets and junk were all missing. In their places were a comfortable-looking cream sofa and a pale blue easy chair. On the wall, a TV that was on. Next to that was a tiny kitchenette area with a fridge, sink, and microwave. On the opposite wall was a tidy desk with a laptop and a small, neat stack of paperwork. On a paper plate by the laptop was a partially eaten sandwich.

"Wow." Madison went over to peer at what looked like an original painting behind the sofa. "Pretty swanky."

"Well, Grandma told me to make myself comfortable out

here." Addie grabbed the remote to turn off the TV and put her sandwich in the little fridge before turning around. "Now, what do you want?"

Madison was still trying to recover from her surprise over the old office's transformation, but she managed to spill out her story about ordering the trees. "The customer service was amazing," she went on. "We even got an extra discount because we're part of the burn area. They really wanted to help us."

"You mean help *you*." Addie folded her arms in front of her. "Don't forget this is your little project, Madison. Not mine."

"I thought we were co-owners here."

"That's true. But this business decision was yours, not mine."

"So I will own the six thousand trees I plan to plant?"

"Six thousand trees?" Addie blinked. "Are you kidding me?"

"Nope."

"How can you possibly get them all planted?"

"It can be done." She told her about the flyer she'd posted at school. "And I put one at Borden's Market too."

"Right . . ." Addie rolled her eyes. "I'm sure those kids will be knocking down the door just to help you."

Madison was starting to feel defensive. "Even if they don't, I can get it done in two weeks by myself." Okay, she suspected that wasn't realistic, but for the sake of argument, she wasn't budging.

"You're unbelievable. Those trees will probably all die by then. What a ridiculous waste of your money."

"I can keep them alive." She crossed her arms. "Anyway, I didn't come in here to argue. I came to ask for your help. Even if we don't get any workers, you and I could knock it out in—"

"Forget it, Madison. Count me out."

"Really? You don't want a part of this? I mean, sure it'll be hard, but think about the value. Do the math, Addie. In less than ten years, those six thousand trees will be worth a small fortune."

"For whoever buys the farm."

"What?" Madison sank down onto the sofa. "What're you saying?"

"We have to sell." Addie sat across from her in the chair, then leaned forward with a serious expression. "It's our *only* option."

"Why?"

"We're steadily going in the hole."

"How's that possible? We still have plenty of trees to sell for this Christmas season. I've seen how many are ready. And more that will be ready in upcoming years. Plus, we still have wreaths to make and sell too. I was about to organize the barn for that."

"Fine, but tell me, who's going to make the wreaths? And who's going to cut and wrap those trees? Who's going to ship them?"

"Haven't you contracted the tree wholesalers by now like Dad always did?"

Addie ignored her question. "Have you noticed how tall our trees have gotten?"

"Sure, but that's not a problem. We just cut them higher."

"The reason they're so tall is we haven't cut them the last *three* years."

"Oh?" Madison considered this. "Well, what about the U-cut season? People come in from town to buy them. And that's when we sell wreaths too."

"The U-cutters were the only thing that brought in money. And there were only a handful of them." Addie sighed. "But it's over, Madison."

"Stop saying that. Dad and Grandma and Grandpa would be—"

"We don't have a choice." Addie stood, holding her hands up in a helpless gesture. "We *have* to sell. The problem is this is a lousy time for real estate around here. Thanks to the fire, too many properties are for sale all up and down the river. Prices are low. I just wanted to hold out long enough to get a fair price. For both of us."

"But I don't *want* to sell. I love the tree farm. It's part of our family's legacy. We can't give it up."

"We can't keep it."

"I don't agree." Madison folded her arms in front of her. "I won't give it up. Not without a fight."

"And how exactly do you plan to fight, Madison?"

"We will turn a profit," she declared.

Addie laughed humorlessly. "Right. Don't you understand that the workforce was scarce enough before, but then the fire came . . . It's too late."

"If you and I can work hard, we can turn this around. I'll find workers somehow. Look how easy it was for me to find seedlings this morning. I just don't think you tried."

Addie's face flushed with anger. "You have no idea what you're talking about."

Madison waved her hand around the cushy office. "I don't know what you do holed up in here day after day, but judging by what's been neglected outside on the farm, I can tell you've done next to nothing out there. That's not trying!"

"Don't judge me." Addie narrowed her eyes. "I was here taking care of Dad and Grandma while you were out globe-trotting and having fun."

Madison pursed her lips, mentally counting to ten like she would when dealing with a belligerent student. "I appreciate that you were here for them," she said gently. "It was probably harder than I realized. But this is a new era, Addie. We can bring the farm back if we just roll up our sleeves and—"

"Do as you like." Addie opened the office door, as in *hint hint.* "Just don't expect any help from me."

Madison didn't know what to say, so she just sadly shook her head and made her exit. What was wrong with Addie? Why had she given up so easily? Or was there something going on here that Madison didn't fully understand? Still, what choice did she have now? She could probably call and cancel the seedling order, but that felt like failure. And Madison just wasn't the type to surrender just like that. Somehow she had to see this through. The tree farm had been born on risks and had made it for almost seventy-five years. They couldn't give up now!

7

For the next week, Madison and Addie were in some kind of standoff. Not that Madison cared particularly since she had a lot to do before her seedlings arrived. For starters, she called several distributors they'd used in the past. The first few were getting trees from a different region, but she finally hit pay dirt with a youth organization that had purchased trees from McDowell's during her gap year.

"You're kidding!" the man exclaimed. "You actually have trees to sell?"

"You bet we do."

"When I called last spring, I was turned down. And then so many local farms got burned out, it was useless to even ask. Selling Christmas trees has been our best method of raising funds, but I'd given up on this year too. This is a real blessing for us!"

"I'm glad." An idea occurred to Madison. "But there might be a catch. Labor's been a challenge. We might need some help cutting and wrapping the trees."

"We can absolutely do that," the man assured her.

She offered him a discount for their help, and after they settled on numbers, prices, and dates, Madison triumphantly took the good news to Addie. "You need to invoice this." She handed the paper to her sister.

"What do you mean?"

"I sold off all these trees." She pointed to the number. "Can you believe it?"

"There's no way we can deliver on this!" Addie stood with fiery eyes and clenched fists. "Why didn't you talk to me first?"

Madison held up her hands. "Okay, before you freak out, listen." She quickly explained how the youth group was going to cut and wrap the trees. "Just like they did the year I helped Dad and Grandpa. And they're not only helping us, we're helping them. See the price break I gave them?"

"But this is valuable inventory for selling the farm." Addie shook the paper in her face. "Don't you get it?"

"*You* don't get it, Addie. I don't *want* to sell the farm."

"And what about our liability?" Addie protested. "Kids can get hurt with the machinery. We could be sued."

"We'll have them sign some sort of agreement. People do that all the time."

She scowled. "You think everything is so simple, but it's not."

"And you think everything is so complicated. Look, if you won't invoice this, I will." She reached for the paper, but Addie snatched it back.

"Never mind. I'll do it," Addie grumbled. "But if we lose everything, don't blame me."

"I am trying to keep that from happening," Madison said slowly, trying to keep from further aggravating her wet blanket sister. "But it'd sure be nice if you were on board."

Addie answered with a growling noise.

Madison's second project was to stake lines about eight feet apart in the burn area. A guide to plant the seedlings in straight rows. It would've been nice to have help with this, but since Addie wasn't even speaking to her, she knew it was pointless to ask. After the lines were in, she went into the barn to make sure everything was in place and ready for wreath construction. Wreath sales weren't as profitable as trees, but their U-cut customers had always enjoyed the opportunity to purchase attractive greenery after they selected their trees. That had always been Grandma's terrain, along with cocoa and cookies and Christmas music and a big bonfire. But judging by the layers of dust on the storage bins, Madison could see no wreaths had been assembled in years. Probably due to Grandma's age and health, along with Addie's lack of enthusiasm.

But at least the supplies were all there—metal wreath forms, florist tape and wire, bolts of Christmassy ribbons, all kinds of pine cones, and lots of other fun things that Grandma had collected over the decades. The wreath-making process always started in late fall, and the girls got to help when they visited at Thanksgiving time. Madison couldn't wait to get started this year. Although she suspected Addie would bail on her.

Madison had kept her phone with her throughout the week, hoping she'd hear from some of the local teens. There had to be someone who wanted to work. But by the weekend, the only phone call she'd received was from the seedling supplier, informing her the tree plugs would arrive Monday morning. And they did.

Feeling like a protective parent, Madison watched the workers unload the pallets in a shady area not far from the burned acreage. As soon as their truck left, she turned on the sprinklers she'd set up and gave the plugs a good soaking. Then she loaded up a burlap planter's bag, slipped the webbed strap over her shoulder, pulled on her work gloves, picked up a clean hoe, and strode out to the boundary between the McDowell's and Thompson's properties. Then, acting like this was something she did every day, she went to work planting the plugs about eight feet apart. By noon, she had a long section planted along the boundary, but compared to what was left, it felt like a drop in the bucket. And her back was already aching. So much for the yoga exercises she'd been doing this week.

After a short lunch break, her back felt better and she was

ready to go again. Her goal was to get trees planted along the whole boundary, but when she heard the rev of Lily's motorbike, she wanted to quit. Maybe Addie was right. Maybe this was a waste of time and money. Madison stood to stretch, peering down the long row of very tiny trees. It would take years before they were big enough to help screen the dust. With hands on hips, she watched the bright blue helmet getting closer and braced herself for the dust cloud that would follow. But the motorbike stopped, and Lily got off and strolled over to Madison with a puzzled expression.

"What're you doing?" she asked.

"Planting Christmas trees." Madison forced a small smile on her face for the pushy girl.

"Oh yeah. They're so small, I didn't even see them. Wow, did you plant all those yourself?"

Madison nodded grimly. "Yep. It's harder work than I remember."

"How long will it take them to grow into real Christmas trees?" Lily undid her helmet strap.

Madison sighed. "About ten years on average, depending on pruning and weather and things."

"Wow, I'll be twenty-one by then."

Madison paused to realize she'd be forty-eight herself. More than middle-aged. This replanting plan suddenly felt wilder than ever.

"How many are you going to plant?" Lily squinted over the blackened acreage.

"Six thousand total."

"No way."

Pursing her lips, she nodded again. "Way."

"All by yourself?"

"Well, I'd hoped for workers." She told Lily about the flyers she'd hung.

"Do you pay much?" Lily tugged off her helmet, shifting her weight to the other foot.

"Fifteen dollars an hour."

Lily's brow creased. "So if I worked ten hours, you'd pay me $150?"

"Your math is right on." Madison studied the girl. "Are you saying you want to work for me?"

"Would you hire me?"

"If you were willing. But I'll warn you, it's hard work."

"I know how to work hard."

"Of course, your dad would have to give permission."

"When could I start?"

Madison blinked. "Whenever you like. I mean, if you're sure you want to do this."

"I want a new dirt bike, and Dad said I have to earn the money myself. But he was only going to pay me ten dollars an hour, and that is gonna be real hard work, like digging and shoveling gravel." She nodded to the hoe in Madison's hand. "That looks kind of easy."

"Want to try it?" Madison held out the tool.

"Can I?"

"Go for it. I'm ready for a break anyway."

Lily traded her helmet for the hoe, and Madison explained how she used an eight-foot string to measure between trees. Then she showed her how to use the hoe to measure the depth of the hole.

"Now you put the plug in up to here." She pointed to the spot on the skinny trunk.

"Are they called plugs 'cause you plug 'em in?" Lily started using her hands to fill the dirt back in.

"It's easier if you use your feet to pack it." Madison showed her how with a couple stomps.

"Can I do another?" Lily asked.

"I guess so." Feeling like Tom Sawyer pulling in Huck Finn, Madison handed Lily another seedling. It wasn't long before Lily had planted several. "You're actually pretty good at this," Madison told her.

"Planting trees is fun. So you'll really hire me? For real?"

"If your dad's okay with it."

"I'll go ask him now." Lily reached for her helmet. "I'll come right back and tell you, okay?"

"Okay with me." As Madison watched Lily zip off, instead of wanting to quit like earlier, she felt surprisingly energized. The girl's enthusiasm seemed to fuel her own. Planting trees *was* fun! Especially if you weren't doing it all on your own. Hopefully Gavin wouldn't mind sharing his daughter with her. Even if Lily didn't work as fast as an adult, having company out here was most welcome! She tucked another seedling into the ground and had just stood up straight to stomp the soil in around it when she heard a male voice calling out a hello. She looked up to see Gavin approaching, alone.

"Hi there." She gave the seedling a couple more stomps. Hopefully he wasn't about to put the kibosh on her wanting to employ child labor.

"Lily tells me you've offered her a job." His brow creased slightly, making it hard to determine his opinion.

"Not a job exactly, just some part-time work. She said she needs to earn money for a new dirt bike."

"That's true." He shoved his hands in his pockets. "I mean, I could just hand it over to her, but what does that teach her? So I suggested she work on the park with me."

"She told me about that."

"But it seems she'd rather work for you."

Madison shrugged. "Is that a problem?"

"No, not exactly."

"She already demonstrated her ability to plant trees." Madison waved down the row. "But I told her she needs your permission."

"Well, if she really wants to do this, I won't stop her." He frowned.

"She told me you have to plant six thousand trees by yourself—is that really true?"

She nodded sheepishly. "Yeah, I may have bitten off too much."

"Maybe so."

"Addie's convinced as much." She peered at him, curious to see if he had any reaction to the mention of her sister's name. "But then she's never been much into actual farmwork."

He smiled. "Yeah, Addie's more of an indoor girl."

"I hear that you and she have gotten to be good friends." She continued to study him. "That's nice."

"Addie's been a good neighbor. And a good friend to Lily."

She slowly nodded. "I also heard you lost your wife," she added quietly. "I'm so sorry, Gavin."

"Thanks." He looked uneasy now. "You know, Madison. I always felt like I should talk to you, you know, about old stuff." He glanced up at the revving sound of a dirt bike approaching. "Lily wanted to grab a snack before she came back to help," he explained. "She wanted to start work today. If that's okay."

"Sure. There are still a couple of good hours left." She watched as Lily came to a fast stop, sending dark dust flying. For some reason it didn't bother her as much now. Maybe because she was already covered in that same kind of black grime herself. She waved to Lily. "I hear I've got my first employee."

"Yeah." Lily set her helmet on her bike. "Dad said it was okay."

"I think you gals got your work cut out for you." He shook his head. "Six thousand trees."

"One tree at a time." Madison handed Lily the hoe and then took off the planter's bag, looping it over Lily's shoulder and handing her the measuring string. "I'll go get more trees and a hoe and be right back."

"If you bring back two hoes, I might like to give it a try," Gavin told her. "Off the clock."

"Seriously?" She pointed to his light khaki pants. "You'll get filthy."

"Wouldn't be the first time." His dark blue eyes twinkled. "Remember me? The guy who didn't mind getting his hands dirty."

"Okay then." As she walked away, she overheard Lily explaining the planting steps to her dad.

Well, this was totally unexpected. She suspected Gavin's only motive for hanging around was to be sure Madison wasn't overworking his daughter. Just being a good parent. But she was curious . . . what had he been about to tell her?

She hurried to the barn and quickly gathered up planter bags, hoes, and measuring strings. Between the three of them, they might get another row started before quitting time. She stopped to fill the bags with trees and, glancing over toward the house, wondered what Addie would think of her recruitment of Lily and Gavin for farmhands. But by the time she got back, only Lily was there.

"Dad got a phone call," Lily told her. "He had to go back to the trailer to work on something."

"Oh?" Madison adjusted the bag's strap on her shoulder and tugged her work gloves back on. "Does he work remotely out here?"

"Huh?" Lily looked up from the seedling she was putting in a hole.

"Does he have a job he does from the trailer?"

"He's a consultant." Lily stood, stomping around the dirt by the baby tree.

"What kind of consulting does he do?" Madison jabbed her hoe into the earth.

"For the business that he sold. He promised the new owners that he'd consult with them for a year. That's why he's busy sometimes. His year is supposed to be up in November. After that, he can really work on our dirt bike park."

"Oh, I see."

"I don't really know what he does as a consultant, but I guess it's pretty important." Lily raised her hoe high, then plunged it deep into the ground. "Because when they call, he's gotta answer."

Madison was actually relieved that Gavin was gone. As much as she needed help, she wasn't sure she was ready to be around him too much. At least not until they had a chance to speak privately. She had a few things she wanted to say to him too!

8

By quitting time, Madison's opinion of Lily had changed completely. Oh, the girl was strong-willed and outspoken and a little rough around the edges, but she was also refreshingly sincere. And a hard worker too.

"I'll come over as soon as I get home from school tomorrow," Lily promised as she handed over her tools.

"Great. And I can pay you as we go, or I can keep track of your hours and pay all at once."

"All at once." Lily tugged her helmet on, shoving wild curls away from her face.

"Got it. And I plan to tell the high school kids, if they ever show, that I'll offer a bonus if they stick around until all the trees are planted. That goes for you too if you want."

"I'll do that." Lily's eyes lit up. "Stick around."

"Great. I'll gladly pay you a bonus. But I'll understand if you need to quit."

"What if high school kids do come? Will you still want me?"

"Of course." Madison patted her on the back. "You're a good planter. I can definitely use your help."

Lily beamed at her.

"But you might get tired of the work or—"

"No, I won't. I'll stick with you until every tree is planted. You'll see. Dad's always telling me that I'm too stubborn."

Madison laughed. "I think he used to say the same thing about me."

Lily cocked her head to one side. "You knew my dad? I mean, before?"

"Oh yeah. All the kids along the river knew each other. We all used to hang out by the water, back when I stayed with my grandparents."

"Did you know my mom too?"

"Not very well. But, yes, I knew her." Madison didn't know what to say. "She was a little older than me . . . and such a pretty girl." She placed her hand on Lily's shoulder. "I'm really sorry for your loss. I'm sure it hasn't been easy."

Lily's nod was somber. "See ya tomorrow." She revved her bike. "Don't plant all those trees without me."

"No worries there." Madison laughed as she waved, then she gathered up the rest of the tools and trudged back to the house. She was exhausted, but it was a good kind of exhausted. She hoped Addie wouldn't mind if she commandeered the old clawfoot tub for herself tonight. Hopefully she could unearth an old bag of Grandma's beloved Epsom salts.

• • •

Faithful to her word, Lily came back the next afternoon. Madison was so tired by then, she'd almost hoped Lily would forget and give her an excuse to call it a day. But having Lily's help and loquacious company lifted Madison's spirits, and the afternoon went by more quickly than expected. Lily was quite a character. Smart as a whip and not afraid to voice her opinions—of which she had many. From music to food to video games, she had something to say about everything. Although the girl did slow down at the end of the workday.

"I hope this hard labor isn't too much for you," Madison said

58

as she watched Lily stomp the soil down around the last tree with much less energy than she had earlier. "I'll totally understand if you need to take a day off—and it won't affect your bonus."

Lily handed the work gloves back to her. "Don't worry, I'm fine." She frowned at her dirty hands. "But I guess I could use a shower. Anyway, that's what Taylor told me at lunch today."

"Who's Taylor?"

"My best friend. Anyway, she says she's my best friend. But she can be kinda mean sometimes." Lily rubbed her nose, making the dark smudge already there even worse.

"I know your trailer's bathroom is pretty tight. You could come to the house to clean up if you want."

"Yeah, Addie lets me do that sometimes. I guess it's not a bad idea."

"And you can stay for dinner if you want. I've got a big batch of stew simmering in the Crock-Pot."

"Can Dad come too?" Lily asked hopefully.

"Of course." Madison tried to act nonchalant. "I mean, if he wants. It's only stew. Nothing fancy."

"Can you call him? I don't have my own phone yet." Lily scowled. "Dad says I have to be twelve first."

Madison fished her phone out of her jeans pocket. "Here."

"Nah, you talk to him." Lily told her the number. "He won't tell you no."

So Madison called and explained the plan.

"That sounds great," he said. "Lily could use a good bath, and I was just wondering what to fix for dinner. Homemade stew sounds awesome."

So it was settled. Madison told him six o'clock, and he promised to bring Lily a clean change of clothes. A wave of nerves rushed over Madison as she and Lily walked to the house. Having Gavin for dinner tonight had not been in her plan. The house was messy, the only thing on the menu was stew, and she and

Addie were not even speaking. All ingredients for an interesting evening.

But after getting Lily set up in the bathroom and herself cleaned up as best she could, she realized that Addie's car was gone. Just the same, she put four settings on the dining room table and even lit a fat candle in the center. Then she put a loaf of frozen sourdough bread in the oven and, feeling apologetic for her bare-bones meal, went ahead and added a few more veggies to the leftover salad she'd made for herself last night. She even threw together a hasty appetizer plate of apple slices, cheese, and crackers.

She'd just set the appetizers on the little kitchen table when she heard Gavin calling out. "Hello! Anyone home? Mind if I let myself in?"

"In the kitchen," she called back.

Looking ruggedly handsome in a western chambray shirt and blue jeans, he held up a bottle of wine in one hand and a paper sack in the other. "Something smells awfully good in here." He grinned.

"Well, it's only stew. My grandma's recipe. But it's been cooking all day, so the meat should be tender." She went to turn down the Crock-Pot. "Autumn seems the perfect time for stew." She didn't mention that she'd made a big batch thinking she'd have it to eat on all week. But, really, wasn't this better? Except for her nerves. At the moment, she wasn't the slightest bit hungry.

"I brought a Pinot Noir from a local winery. I hope that's okay." He looked directly into her eyes with an intensity that caught her off guard.

"It's, uh, it's okay with me." She felt her cheeks warm as she stepped back, steadying herself. Was it her imagination or was he sending her signals?

He turned and set the wine next to the appetizers. "Is Lily still cleaning up?"

"I think so." She suddenly wished she'd taken more time to fix herself up better. Although Gavin didn't appear to mind.

He patted the paper sack. "I'll go put her clothes by the bath-room door."

As he left, she went in search of a corkscrew and wineglasses . . . and tried to calm herself. Really, this was no big deal. Just neighbors sharing a meal. Nothing more. She glanced out the window, curious as to when Addie would return . . . and how she would react to this impromptu dinner party. The oven timer buzzed, and she jumped. She reminded herself to relax, and just as she was removing the sourdough from the oven, Gavin came back. As she set it out to cool, he opened and poured the wine.

"That looks good." He nodded to the bread as he handed her a glass. "A loaf of bread, a jug of wine, and . . ." He chuckled, and her cheeks grew warmer.

"Thanks." She forced a nervous smile. "Here's to neighbors."

He held up his glass. "And to old friends."

She clinked her glass with his. "To old friends."

His eyes twinkled.

As they both took a sip, she considered the words she wanted to say. Something she'd been rehearsing since yesterday. Something like: "I know we parted awkwardly as teens . . . and there were some unspoken things between us . . . but I want you to know I realize that is all in the past . . . water under the bridge . . . no hard feelings." Or something to that lighthearted effect. Something to wipe it all away. But looking at him now, the words evaporated right before her. So she set down her glass and began to slice the still-warm bread.

"Let me do that." Gavin reached for the knife. "You must be tired."

She easily surrendered. "Thanks. I guess I am."

"I'm really glad you came back here," Gavin said as he sliced. "I honestly didn't ever expect to see you again."

"Really?" She considered this. "Even though my family owns the property next to yours? You never thought we'd cross paths again?"

"Maybe I thought you wouldn't want us to . . ."

She wasn't sure how to respond.

"I realize we parted ways pretty suddenly," he continued. "You know, way back when." His brow furrowed. "I've always felt badly."

"We were . . . young," she said lamely.

"For sure." He nodded, turning his attention back to the bread. "It was a long time ago, but seeing you again sort of brought it all back." He looked up with a curious expression that seemed to beg a better response from her.

"Yes, I was surprised to see you after all these years," she stammered.

"I hope it's a good surprise." His dark brows arched hopefully.

"Yes, of course." She smiled weakly. Could this feel any more awkward?

"When Lily and I moved back here, I talked to Addie, and she made it sound like you were determined to live abroad for the rest of your days. Like you'd left the country for good."

Madison shrugged. "I suppose I might've given everyone that idea at one time. But plans change."

"That's for sure." He set down the knife. "Addie also suggested you might be married. Weren't you engaged to a fellow teacher over there in Mongolia? Another world traveler?"

"Not exactly engaged. I suppose I thought we would be eventually. But it sort of . . . unraveled." She took a nervous sip. How had this turned personal so quickly? She focused on placing slices into the bread basket. Then, feeling his eyes on her, she looked up to see that same intensity in his eyes.

"Well, I'm sorry."

"Sorry?" She picked up the bread basket to take to the dining room.

"For the guy's sake." He followed her. "Maybe he didn't have good sense? I mean, to let you slip away so easily."

She couldn't help but smile at the irony. "Actually, it was his choice. Mostly, anyway. After it was all said and done, I realized it was for the best." She heard footsteps approaching and, assuming it was Addie, braced herself. To her relief it was just Lily coming down the stairs, still towel-drying her hair. Her freshly washed skin pink.

"I'm starved," Lily announced, helping herself to some crackers and cheese. "When do we eat?"

"Right now if you like." Madison tousled the girl's damp curls. "Your hair is so pretty."

"Ugh. It's a pain." Lily popped an apple slice into her mouth.

"Isn't Addie joining us?" Gavin glanced toward the living room.

"She's not here," Madison answered. "I don't know where she went, but her car's gone. I'm sure she won't mind if we start without her." Madison didn't feel like mentioning that she and Addie rarely shared a meal together anyway. "I'll dish up the stew while you—"

"Let me do that," Gavin offered. "After all, you two were the hard workers today. You ladies go sit down."

"Okay." She and Lily took their chairs, making small talk until Gavin brought out the steaming bowls. When he finally sat down, he bowed his head and prayed a quick but genuine blessing, even expressing thanks for a rediscovered friendship. Madison couldn't help but smile. The homey scene was sweetly touching. *This is how people should live*, she thought as she laid her napkin in her lap.

"You're making good progress with the tree planting." Gavin passed her the salad bowl. "I'm impressed."

"There's still so many trees left." Madison sighed. "I'm trying not to be overwhelmed every time I see the plugs on the pallets."

"I would've come to help today, but I had a super long Zoom meeting and some complications. I don't have anything scheduled for tomorrow, so if it's okay, I'd like to give you a hand."

"Okay? That'd be fantastic." She buttered a slice of bread.

"I haven't planted trees for quite a while, but I'm sure it'll come back to me."

"That's right. You used to help with the hazelnut orchard."

"Hazelnuts?" Lily's brows shot up. "I thought they were filberts."

Madison laughed. "That's always been a controversial subject along the river."

"I grew up on a filbert farm," Gavin declared. "But somewhere along the way, it became more correct to call them hazelnuts. I'm not even sure why. But I never stopped calling them filberts."

"Will you ever plant any more nut trees?" Madison asked. "I mean, just for fun. For family history?"

"That's not a bad idea. I definitely want to plant trees for shade and whatnot. Bigger than seedlings though. We need to green up the place some."

"Yeah, we have lots of trees drawn into our plans for the bike park," Lily chimed in.

"Tell me more about your ideas for the park." Madison had been trying to hold back her judgment. Although she still disliked the idea of living next to such a noisy place, there was nothing she could do about it. She wanted to be as open as possible, so she listened patiently as Lily enthusiastically described the trails and hills and obstacles—every detail down to where the little camp cabins would be situated alongside the river.

"And maybe even a swimming pool," she added. "Right, Dad?"

"It's open for consideration. Although I've always preferred the river myself." He winked at Madison. "Remember the good times we had down there?"

She nodded. "But with all the fallen trees from the fire, it might not be too safe for a while. You know, with branches to catch you and changing undercurrents."

"Yeah." He rubbed his beard. "We sure don't want anyone to get hurt."

"And where will you guys live?" Madison asked. "In one of the cabins?"

"No way." Lily shook her head. "Dad already drew plans for our house."

"I only sketched a rough draft," he corrected. "An architect took it from there. It's a simple design. But enough for us. With high ceilings, a big fireplace, and everything overlooking the river."

"Sounds lovely." Madison had often wished her grandparents' home was closer to the river, but Grandpa had worried about flooding back in the days before dams were built. "When will you start construction?"

"Any day now, I hope. The permits were just approved. My contractor expects it to be done by next spring."

They continued to visit while they ate, but when they were done and still sitting at the table, Gavin pointed to his daughter. "Okay, young lady, I'm pretty sure you have homework to do."

Lily rolled her eyes, and Gavin pulled a small flashlight out of his pocket. "Why don't you get yourself back to the trailer and get started on it while I help Madison clean up the dinner things."

"Yeah, yeah . . ." Lily took the flashlight, gathered up her bag of dirty clothes, and trudged off. But Madison and Gavin remained at the table. Neither one speaking. The candle flickered warmly, and Madison realized her earlier nervousness had completely vanished. In fact, she was wishing this moment could just keep going.

"I'm sorry I didn't plan any dessert," she told him. "Although I do have some ice cream in the freezer if you—"

"No thanks. How about we finish this off for dessert." He lifted the bottle and refilled her glass.

"Okay." She smiled. "It's very good."

"A friend of mine owns the vineyard. It's about five miles up-river from here. Just beyond where the fire started. He was lucky to be spared."

She studied the bottle's label. "Yes, I've heard of this vineyard."

She leaned back in her chair. "Things were really starting to change around here before I left. Too bad the fire ruined it for so many."

"It'll come back." He held up his glass to her. "Thanks to dreamers like you. Look what you've already accomplished and you're barely back." He leaned forward. "I'm curious, Madison, how long do you plan to stay?"

"Oh." She considered this. "Well, I thought I'd come home. Maybe for good . . . although Addie seems to have other plans."

His brow creased. "What kind of plans?"

"She wants to sell the farm."

"Sell the family tree farm? Why?"

"Apparently it's been losing money."

"But you're planting all those trees. Things will turn around."

"I guess I'm making my last-ditch effort to see if we can save it." She grimaced. "And to be honest, it was also to create some separation from your dirt bike park."

"Oh?" He set his glass down. "So you're still not a fan of Lily's plan."

She shrugged. "The thought of noisy engines and dust is not that appealing."

He reached forward to gather the dishes. "I know it's not ideal, but it's her dream." He set the stack of dishes to one side and released a long sigh. "Lily has already had so much loss in her young life . . . it might seem silly to some people, but it's something I really want to give her."

Madison felt guilty now. "I understand," she said quietly. "And it'll probably be a great destination for kids and families."

"But not so good for neighbors?" He looked intently into her eyes.

She glanced away. "I guess time will tell."

"To good neighbors?" He looked hopeful as he held up his wine.

She smiled, clinking her glass against his. "To good neighbors."

Once again, she heard the sound of footsteps, but this time, it was Addie. Framed in the door to the living room with her hands on her hips, Addie stared at them with a frosty expression.

"Well, this is certainly cozy." She strode into the room with arched brows. "Am I interrupting something?"

Madison set down her glass with a clunk. "No, of course not. We just finished dinner and—"

"I didn't realize you were entertaining tonight." Addie gripped the back of a chair with a scrutinizing expression.

"Well, it was pretty spur-of-the-moment. Just Lily and Gavin." Madison pointed to the unused place setting. "We thought maybe you'd join us, but you were gone."

"I drove to town for a bite and some shopping."

"Right." Madison stood, helping Gavin to gather the dishes.

"You missed out on a great meal." Gavin led the way to the kitchen.

"There's still stew." Madison turned the Crock-Pot off.

"Beef stew," Addie pointed out. "Which I can't eat."

"Oh, yeah." Gavin set the dishes in the sink. "I forgot you're a vegetarian."

"Everyone seems to forget that." Addie locked eyes with Madison. "I realize I'm such an inconvenience."

Madison didn't know what to say.

Gavin put a hand on Madison's shoulder. "Well, thank you for a delicious dinner. And like I said, I'll be over to plant trees tomorrow."

"You're kidding," Addie exclaimed. "You actually plan to help with Madison's bizarre scheme?"

"It's not so bizarre." Gavin grinned at Madison.

"Six thousand trees and no labor . . . yeah, right." Addie's dismissive tone was chilling. Almost like she wanted Madison to fail.

Eager to escape her sister's foul mood, Madison followed Gavin to the front door to say goodbye. It wasn't exactly how she wanted the evening to end, but up until wet-blanket Addie had arrived, it was enough to give her hope.

Of course, she still had Addie to face. That might prove dicey. As Madison closed the front door behind Gavin, she wondered if there was some way to pick up the pieces and patch things up with her sister.

9

Madison didn't know whether to be relieved or concerned when Addie made herself scarce when she returned to the kitchen to finish cleaning up the dinner things. But by the time she headed to bed, she was too tired to care. And the next morning, Addie silently got her coffee and disappeared into her comfy office. Well, fine. If she wanted to be childish, she'd let her. Madison had better things to do than fret over Addie's bad attitude.

As promised, Gavin came to help, but the conversation between them was limited to the work, and by the time they broke for lunch, Madison felt awkward. When she returned to planting, she was relieved that he hadn't come back yet and almost hoped he wouldn't. For whatever reason, things felt awkward between them now.

When Lily came home from school, she told Madison that her dad had gotten another urgent phone call and probably wouldn't make it back to help. As they worked together, Madison was grateful for Lily's lighthearted chatter and youthful energy. But when they quit, she felt apologetic. "Look, Lily," she said. "You're a kid, and I don't really expect you to work like this in all your spare time. I'm sure you must have things to do."

Lily frowned. "You don't want my help?"

"No, of course not. I love your help. But I don't want to take all your time. And don't worry about the bonus. I'll still—"

"But I like working here." She continued walking back to the barn with Madison.

"Okay, good," Madison said. "I just don't want you to feel pressured."

"I'm just glad I'm going to get my new bike. The way I have it figured, I'll have earned enough by the end of next week to afford it. I mean, if you have enough work. You do, don't you?"

Madison shook her hoe at the still huge pile of plugs. "No worries there." At the moment her only concern was how many of the seedlings would die before she got them into the ground. Despite keeping them damp, some were starting to look a little weary.

As they laid their tools down, Lily pointed to the barn. "That's such a cool building. It's like something you'd see in a movie."

"It's almost seventy-five years old."

"What do you use it for? I mean, it's not like you have horses or cows."

Madison laughed. "It's mostly for storage and wreath making."

"Christmas wreaths?"

Madison explained about her grandmother's little side business, showing her all the nails along the side of the barn. "She hung them out here. It always looked so pretty."

"Will you do that this year?"

"I hope so." Madison dusted off her sooty hands on her jeans.

"Can I see inside?"

Madison shrugged. "Sure. Why not?"

She turned on the lights and showed Lily the wreath-making area, and the girl was suitably impressed. "Will you need help with this too?"

"You think you'll still want to work for me by then?"

Lily nodded eagerly.

"Then of course."

"This barn is so cool." Lily strolled about. "It'd be perfect for a harvest party."

Madison looked around. "Yeah, I guess it would."

"Have you ever thrown one before?"

"No, I wasn't usually here that time of year."

"We have some friends back home where we used to live. They had a barn kinda like this, and they always had this big harvest party with music and dancing and food. It was so fun." Lily sighed. "I'm gonna miss it."

Madison considered this. Already she was tired and overwhelmed with tree planting, but part of her was intrigued. "That does sound fun . . . but it would be a lot of work."

"I'd help you," Lily offered. "And I bet Taylor would too. Maybe some of my other friends. You could invite all the neighbors."

"Tell you what, I'll think about it. But until I get the seedlings planted, it's hard to imagine doing anything else."

"Yeah." Lily sighed. "Dad's always telling me not to bite off more than I can chew."

Madison grinned. How many times had she heard that herself?

"I better go." Lily opened the door. "I have to write a book report, and if I don't keep my grades up, the dirt bike park won't happen."

Madison thanked her again, and they parted ways. She was just latching the barn door when she heard footsteps crunching in the gravel behind her.

"Sounds like you're getting pretty friendly with Lily," Addie said as she joined her.

"She's a good kid." Madison studied her sister in the dusky light. "So you're speaking to me now?"

"I wasn't *not* speaking to you."

Madison started for the house. "Could've fooled me."

"Well, can you blame me for feeling a little put out?"

Madison glanced at her. "Put out?"

"Well, it's like you show up out of the blue, then you push me aside and take over."

"Seriously?" Madison tried to suppress the defensive feeling rising in her. All she was doing was trying to help. And it was hard work. But was Addie the least bit grateful?

"Yeah, I've been running things just fine on my own."

"Really?" Madison knew she needed to bite her tongue.

"It wasn't easy helping Dad and Grandma . . . and losing them while you were off having fun." Addie stomped up the front steps.

"Having fun? I was working hard and—"

"I read the letters you wrote Grandma. Sure sounded like you were having fun."

"Well, I probably wanted to cheer her up—make it sound better than it was."

Addie opened the door. "Anyway, that's not my point."

"What is your point then?"

Addie stopped in the doorway, arms crossed. "I don't like you pushing me aside and taking over."

"How exactly have I pushed you aside and taken over?" Madison wanted to push her aside right now to get in the house but remained on the front stoop. "I realize you think we should sell the farm, but I told you I'm not ready to give up so easily. Are you saying that me using my own money and my time to plant trees is taking over? Can't you see that what I'm doing actually increases the property value in the event we do sell—and if we don't sell, it's an investment in our future?"

"It's not just that. It's like you're endearing yourself to Gavin and Lily now."

She didn't expect that. "What?"

"I know what you're doing." Addie's face was grim. "You knew that I was interested in Gavin, Madison. So you're trying to win over Lily to get to him."

"Are you kidding?" Now, Madison did push past her sister. Peeling off her sooty sweatshirt, she turned to stare at her. "For your information, Gavin and I used to be—well, we were good friends. And now that we're neighbors again, well, it's only natural to rekindle that friendship." She felt her cheeks warming from the heat in the house . . . or something else.

"That's not what it looked like to me last night." Addie's blue eyes looked fiery. "Do you know how that made me feel? To walk in on you like that?"

"We were just finishing up a simple little impromptu dinner. Nothing more."

"With wine and candlelight?" Addie stepped closer, peering up into Madison's face.

She just shook her head. "You're overblowing the whole thing."

"Really? You can look me in the eye and deny that you're interested in him?"

"Oh, Addie, you're being ridiculous. And I'm tired." Madison tried to push past her again.

"I want to know, Madison—are you interested in Gavin? Because I already told you that I thought there was something between him and me, and now you stroll up and, just like when we were kids, you just take over and ruin everything for me." Addie looked close to tears. "I wish you'd stayed in Mongolia."

Madison didn't know what to say. Should she confess that she and Gavin had once been in a relationship? That he'd broken her heart? That she still felt an attraction to him? What good would that do? Especially if Gavin didn't share those feelings. To be fair, she wasn't positive he did. She could've misread his signals. Hadn't she done that once before? And then he'd dumped her for a girl very much like Addie. Why should she imagine that couldn't happen again?

"Tell me," Addie pressed, "are you after Gavin?"

"No, I'm not *after* Gavin," she answered evenly.

"Really?" Addie reached for Madison's hand. "You wouldn't lie to me, would you?"

Madison pursed her lips. That hadn't really been a lie. She wasn't pursuing him or chasing *after* him. "I'm just *after* some food and a shower," she said. "And a good night's sleep."

"So you're not using Lily to get to him?"

"No, of course not!" Madison frowned. "I can't believe you'd suggest I'd do something like that."

"I'm sorry, Madison." Addie's sigh sounded slightly aggravated. "Maybe you're right. Maybe I did overblow the whole thing."

Madison was taken aback by the apology. Was it sincere?

"It's just that I used to have a giant crush on Gavin back when we were kids."

"Really?" Madison tried to wrap her head around this. "But he's, what, six years older than you."

"I know. But remember that summer when I lost Charlie?"

"Charlie the Chihuahua?" Madison grimaced to think of the yippy little dog that Addie had insisted she had to have for her tenth birthday, but then neglected. To the point that Mom eventually found a new home for the poor thing—and Addie barely noticed.

"Yes. Charlie the Chihuahua. Remember how he got lost that one summer here on the farm? Dad was certain coyotes got him."

Madison gave a slight nod. Dad had probably hoped coyotes had gotten him.

"Remember how Gavin drove me all around? And how he helped me to find Charlie? It was so sweet and kind."

"As I recall, Gavin helped *me* find Charlie." Madison flashed back to that hot summer night. Gavin had driven her up and down the river road while she called and whistled for the lost dog. "Then we finally found him down by the boat ramp . . . around midnight." Okay, maybe it had been earlier in the evening, but she and Gavin celebrated with a jump in the river and a make-out session afterward. And since they came home with the dog, she didn't even get in trouble for being out so late.

"Okay, maybe you did find him, but Gavin had been helping me look for Charlie all day long. He drove me around in his truck and even bought me a Fudgsicle to cheer me up. He was so sympathetic and concerned about me."

"Right." Madison had no desire to dispute this.

"Even though I was only ten, I was mature for my age. And I had the biggest crush on him that summer."

"Uh-huh." Madison frowned. "And what's your point exactly?"

Addie smiled. "Just that I had first dibs."

"First dibs? Seriously?"

Addie's lower lip protruded. "Yeah. And maybe if I had been older, he wouldn't have married Shelby."

Madison couldn't help but roll her eyes. "Right."

"I know you think I'm being silly. And maybe I am a little, but I'm also being honest. I wish you could respect that."

"Fine. I respect that. Okay?" Madison held up her filthy hands, hoping to end this frustrating conversation. "I need to go get cleaned up."

"Maybe we've never been close. But we're sisters, Madison. And sisters should respect each other's territory. *Right?*"

Madison was speechless now. So Gavin was Addie's territory? She was tempted to spill out her own sad story and mark her territory, but the words scrambled and tangled inside of her. Plus, she was just plain tired.

"So we're okay now?" Addie smiled, opening her arms for a hug. "You still love your baby sis?"

Madison hugged her, but now feeling both mentally and physically exhausted, she excused herself to go clean up. Dibs, really? What were they, thirteen?

10

Gavin showed up bright and early to help Madison plant the next morning. He even apologized for bailing on her the previous day. "I didn't realize it would take so long to figure things out. But today should be interruption free for me."

"No worries if it's not. I understand. And I really appreciate your help." She plunked a seedling into the hole he'd just made, then filled the dirt back in and tamped it down with her feet while he moved on to make the next hole. This was a new system that he'd suggested—he'd be the digger and she the filler. And she had no complaints since she was getting the easier part of the deal.

"Lily sure enjoys working with you," he told her. "I'm glad you don't mind her constant chatter."

"Not at all. It helps pass the time. She's actually pretty interesting."

"Yeah, in an offbeat sort of way." He chuckled as he plunged his hoe into the black dirt, then glanced toward the house at the sound of a car engine. "Looks like Addie's off somewhere. In a hurry too."

She looked up to see Addie's little blue car making a fast dusty trail down the graveled driveway. "Yeah, I guess so." She pulled another plug from her bag, waiting as he finished digging the hole.

"I'm surprised she's not helping you plant."

"Oh, Addie's never been a big fan of hard labor." She dropped the plug in. "Besides that, she's not really in favor of replanting."

"Why not?"

Madison explained Addie's hopes to sell in the spring. "Well, unless I can prove that we can be profitable."

"I don't see why you can't be profitable." He pointed to the section of healthy Christmas trees. "Just look at all that inventory."

She told him about the tree contract she'd made with the youth organization. "It's not a huge amount of money, but it's better than nothing."

They continued to work, moving quickly together down a long row. It was just a little past noon when Madison's phone rang. She didn't recognize the number but answered anyway.

"Is this the McDowell's Christmas Tree Farm?" a female voice asked.

"Yes. This is Madison McDowell. Can I help you?"

"I'm calling about the poster you put up at my school. You still need help?"

"Yes." Madison felt a surge of hope.

"Great! My name's Clover Wallace and I'm sixteen. My brother, Will, is fifteen, and we've never planted trees before, but we really need to make some money."

"Well, tree planting's pretty simple." As Madison briefly described the process, she saw her sister return and park her car near the edge of the burn area. Then she called out to Gavin to come help her with something.

"It doesn't sound too difficult," Clover said on the phone.

"Yeah, it's definitely not complicated," Madison assured her as she peeled off a filthy glove and watched Gavin cross the farm. "But it is physical labor. And you'll get really dirty."

"We're hard workers," Clover said. "But we can only work after school and on weekends."

"That's fine. And your parents are okay with this?"

"Yeah. It's just our mom. She had to quit her job because of her back." Clover explained about an absent dad who wasn't helping them much. "So you see, we kinda really need to make some money. And babysitting doesn't pay much."

"Well, I really need some good workers." She watched as Gavin climbed into Addie's car. "So if you don't mind getting dirty, come on out and give it a try."

It was agreed that Clover and Will would ride the school bus to the tree farm after school, and Madison would give them a ride home at the end of the day. She hung up her phone, then looked over to see that Addie had driven off with Gavin in tow. She dropped a seedling into the last hole, stomped it into place, then decided it was lunchtime, so she laid down her tools and walked back to the house.

She was curious what Addie and Gavin were up to but didn't want to appear overly nosy, so she simply went in through the kitchen door and washed up. She'd already offered Gavin some lunch as a thank-you for helping, but when she didn't see him anywhere, she wasn't sure if he was still interested. Just the same, she started to grill a pair of ham and cheese sandwiches and opened a can of lentil soup. But when Gavin never showed, she sat down to her own lunch alone. By the time she finished up and put the extra sandwich in the fridge, she was even more curious about Gavin's whereabouts. What was Addie up to?

"Oh, there you are," Addie said as Madison came down the front porch steps a little while later. "I'd been calling for you. I thought you were still out planting."

"I was having lunch in the kitchen." Madison looked over to where some kind of takeout meal was laid out on the picnic table under the pine trees. There was even a checkered tablecloth and a cheery bouquet of sunflowers. Gavin was already seated and smiling toward her.

"I wanted to surprise you guys with lunch, Madison," Addie said. "I got barbecued chicken and several yummy side dishes and even apple pie for dessert. Gavin helped me unload it from the car and set it all up."

Madison frowned. "Wish I'd known. I went in through the back door and didn't see you guys around anywhere. And now I've already had lunch."

"Too bad," Addie chirped. "Well, I'll tell Gavin not to wait then. Catch ya later."

"Yeah." Madison waved to Gavin, then turned away, heading back to planting. She wanted to ask Addie why she hadn't simply called Madison's phone but didn't want to make a fuss. Addie was obviously glad to have Gavin to herself. So be it. Madison had other things to attend to.

Encouraged that she'd have more willing workers after three, Madison went to work. If Gavin preferred Addie's company to hers, Madison didn't care . . . did she? Okay, maybe she did . . . just a little. And when he finally did return to help, she tried to act perfectly normal, like she hadn't minded feeling left out. She didn't even mention that she'd made him lunch. She simply let it go.

"I've got some high school kids coming to work this afternoon," she said brightly, explaining about Clover and Will. "Sounds like they really need jobs."

"You said the last name is Wallace?"

"Yes. Do you know them?"

"I went to school with Mike Wallace. Maybe the kids are related to him."

"Was that the same Mike who used to hang with us at the river in the summertime? The loudmouth who was such a show-off?"

"That sounds like Mike Wallace, but I haven't seen him in years."

Madison told him what Clover had said about her father's lack of support. "So if they turn out to be his kids, I hope they're not like their wild dad."

Gavin laughed. "I don't know. Wild, energetic kids might prove to be good workers."

She smiled as she stomped a seedling into place. "That's something I always appreciated about you, Gavin. You're such an optimist. You always have a good attitude and are looking for the best in people . . . that silver lining."

"Well, thanks, but you know I owe some of that to your grandpa, right?"

"Really? What do you mean?"

"My dad was so busy with the filbert farm and my own grandpa passed away when I was a kid. Your grandpa used to sort of mentor me. Took me under his arm at times. And he was always so positive. I know it really impressed me."

"He was upbeat, wasn't he?" She studied Gavin for a moment. "I never really thought about it before, but you might've known Grandpa better than I did. I mean, you lived here year-round. I only had summers and holidays. And those were such busy times."

"I remember when he told me about the first Christmas tree."

"The Martin Luther story?"

"Yep. How Martin Luther was walking through the woods somewhere in Germany and saw starlight coming through an evergreen tree." He plunged the hoe deep into the soil. "How it was symbolic."

She nodded as she pushed the plug down deep. "Yes, Luther taught that the evergreen tree reaching up to the sky was to point us to God. The stars, which we represent with lights, are to remind us Jesus is the light of the world." How many times had she heard that story as a child? She pulled another seedling from her planter's bag. "It's amazing to think this little sprout will grow up to be a big Christmas tree in someone's home someday." She held it in the air. "God bless whoever gets this tree."

He laughed, then said a hearty "Amen!"

"I can remember Grandpa saying things like that," she said respectfully. "I didn't think much of it then, but suddenly I get it."

"Maybe because you're actually planting trees?"

"Maybe so. It really does make me feel sort of connected to him."

"I asked Addie about wanting to sell the place," he said quietly. "I hope you don't mind. But I was curious."

"I don't mind. What did she say?"

"Just that it was too much for her to manage."

"Even though I'm helping now?"

"I guess she doesn't think you're serious. Or that you'll stay on."

Madison stood up straight. "Really? She said that?"

"Yeah. She thinks you'll get the travel bug again. That you'll leave her high and dry."

"But I told her I was here to stay."

"And the fire really shook her up," he continued. "I know it was scary for everyone. My sister—you remember Mindy? Well, she and Brad had been running the filbert farm. They'd had a rough time with blights and bugs already. They were just getting the upper hand when the fire hit. Naturally, that undid them too. They gave up after that."

"That's understandable when you lose everything like your family did. But the tree farm is still mostly intact. To me it's worth saving."

"Too bad Addie feels differently."

"Yeah." She wanted to add that Addie had different thoughts about a lot of things. Including Gavin. She considered her words. "I think it's nice how you've befriended her. I know how much she's appreciated having you and Lily next door."

"She's been a good neighbor to us too."

Madison had no response, so they both just worked quietly side by side for a while, falling into an easy rhythm of him sinking the hoe into the earth and her following with the plug and seedling. Occasionally they'd pause to get a drink of water or to stretch their muscles. But overall, there was very little conversation.

Clover and Will showed up shortly after Lily came over to

work. Madison could tell by Lily's grim expression that she felt threatened by the new help.

"Hey, how about you show Clover and Will the ropes?" Madison asked her. "You can be like the foreman. Get them all set and show them how it's done."

"Okay." Lily nodded eagerly. "Come on, you guys," she said, addressing the teens. "I'll show you where the tools and stuff are."

As Lily led the siblings away, Gavin winked at Madison. "Nice move. Lily is naturally bossy. She'll enjoy helping like that."

"Well, she's been my most loyal worker so far. Seems only fair."

When Lily and the new workers returned, Addie was with them, wearing overalls and gloves and with a hoe in hand.

"What are you doing here?" Madison asked with astonishment.

"What does it look like?" Addie pointed at Gavin. "You asked me why I wasn't helping. Why don't you show me how it's done?"

He grinned at her. "Glad to."

"Why don't you take over for me." Madison looped a strap of her planter's bag over Addie's shoulder. "Gavin makes the holes, and you fill them."

"Okay." Addie adjusted the heavy bag's weight.

"I'll go back for another load of trees," Madison said as she left. But knowing there were enough seedlings out there to last awhile, she took her time by going into the house for a little break to cool down. Not because she was actually overheated, but to cool off her attitude toward her baby sister. Addie was up to something besides work. She was obviously out there marking her territory right now. And Madison had no intention of getting in her way.

11

Thanks to Clover and Will, several other high school kids, Gavin and Lily, and occasional spurts of energy from Addie—though only when Gavin was working—Madison's six thousand seedlings were all planted in the ground. And it only took two weeks. To celebrate this amazing feat, and thanks to Lily convincing the other teen workers to help her with the planning and setup, Madison agreed to hold a harvest party.

The kids straightened up the barn, hung lights, and set out pumpkins and cornstalks. Clover even persuaded her uncle and his bluegrass band to provide music—for free. Madison's part was to provide food. According to Lily, the menu should include hot dogs and chili and apple cider. "Like my friends' party back home."

Neighbors from along the river and a few acquaintances from town, as well as lots of friends of Lily and the teenagers, all came to the party. A clear evening with a full golden moon provided the perfect backdrop, and everyone was in good spirits. Even Addie seemed to appreciate the informal gathering. Stylishly if not somewhat overly attired in a silky purple dress, Addie played the part of hostess. She seemed to enjoy flitting from guest to guest, although she was mostly focused on Gavin.

Clearly marking her territory as she claimed him for her dance partner again and again.

Meanwhile Madison oversaw the food preparation and serving. Tending the steaming cast-iron pot of spicy chili, she knew she smelled of garlic and onions, but it had to be done. It was also up to her to ensure the hot dogs and fixings remained plentiful. The tasks kept her pleasantly busy. Too busy to change out of her old jeans and flannel shirt before the party started. She'd laid out clean clothes with the hopes of grabbing a shower and taking her hair out of the two pigtail braids. But when it was all said and done, she realized most of the guests were casually dressed too. After all, it was a barn party.

She'd just gone to the kitchen for a couple more gallons of apple cider when she heard the squeak of the screened back door. She was surprised to see Gavin coming in behind her with a slightly furtive expression, like he was hiding from something or someone.

"Good. I could use some help." She handed him a cider jug.

"And I could use a break." He sighed.

"Oh, sorry. I can take that." She reached for the jug.

"Not a physical break." He grimaced as he held fast to the jug. "It's your sister."

Madison couldn't help but chuckle. "I noticed she's been dogging your heels."

"I'm afraid I've given her the wrong idea somehow."

"That's possible." She held up her cider jug. "I really should get these to the barn. We were running low, and it's pretty warm in there. Folks will be thirsty."

He took the jug from her. "I'll take these if you promise to give me a bit of your time."

"Sure." She shrugged.

"And a dance?" he added as they went outside.

"Okay. But let me make sure there's still enough food. Although I think most have eaten by now." She felt a rush of nerves as they walked to the barn. Was this attention just his usual neighborly friendliness or something more? Or was she just his handy excuse to avoid Addie? Which could be problematic considering how things between her and Addie had recently smoothed out some. Madison didn't really want to rock that boat again. Or did she?

Gavin set the cider on the refreshment table while Madison checked to see that the food table was still plentiful. The music played loudly as she followed Gavin out a side door. She didn't look back but wondered if Addie was watching.

"It's quieter out here," Gavin said as he led the way toward the river. "Easier to talk."

"Yeah. The music is great for dancing, but so loud I couldn't hear myself think." She breathed in the cool night air. "It's really mild for late October."

"We should enjoy it. According to this year's *Farmer's Almanac*, we're in for a cold winter."

"You read *Farmer's Almanac*?"

"Of course. Don't you? It was your grandpa that got me hooked on it long ago. It's surprisingly accurate."

"Yeah, but you're not even a farmer anymore."

"I can still care about the weather," he said, defending himself. As they neared the river, Gavin pointed upward. "Check that out."

"A harvest moon." She smiled. "Perfect for our harvest party."

"Actually, it's a hunter's moon."

"Huh?"

"Harvest moon is in September."

"Did you learn that in the *Farmer's Almanac* too?" She elbowed him teasingly.

"Maybe." He winked. "Anyway, the moon is perfect for tonight."

"I totally agree." They both stood quietly, admiring the moon's golden reflection in the ripples of the river. "I'm so glad Lily pushed me to do this party," she said finally. "It's been a little work, but the kids helped a lot. And it's so worth it."

"And just what this community needed. A real morale booster to bring folks together after the fire." He brushed pine needles from the bench that overlooked the river. "Care to sit?"

"Thank you." She sat down gingerly, trying not to feel overly anxious about the very romantic setting. "I probably smell like chili," she apologized. "I never had time to freshen up or change clothes earlier."

"I think you look perfect." He tweaked one of her braids as he took the seat next to her. "Like a farm girl."

She laughed. "Thanks a lot."

He slipped an arm along the back of the bench, turning toward her. "I don't know what to do, Madison."

She felt her heart flutter. Was he about to kiss her? "Do? About what?"

"About Addie."

"Oh, yes. Addie." She took a steadying breath, corralling her thoughts. "Well, as you may have figured out, our Addie is very much into you, Gavin. You'd have to be completely oblivious not to have noticed."

"I've noticed." His tone was solemn. "My question is what do I do about it?"

"Maybe the bigger question should be how do you feel about it?"

He rubbed his bearded chin. "Well, naturally I'm flattered. Addie is an intelligent and beautiful woman. And she's been kind-hearted toward us, always trying to help with Lily." He chuckled. "Although I might appreciate that more than my tomboy daughter does." He looked at Madison. "Lily reminds me of you. Strong-willed, independent, stubborn." His tone was gentle, but it was hard to discern if his comparison was meant to be a compliment or not.

"Well, Lily and I definitely have some things in common," she spoke quietly. "But we were talking about Addie . . . and how you feel."

"Right. It's a fair question. To be honest, this is sort of new to me, Madison. I mean, I haven't dated anyone since . . . well, since I was a kid. And barely then." He folded his arms in front of him and, leaning forward, gazed out over the river with a faraway look. Neither of them spoke for a long moment. She glanced at the part of the old oak tree where she knew their initials were still barely visible, though thankfully not in this dim light. She watched Gavin from the corner of her eye, waiting, wondering if he remembered being here with her, sometimes on this very bench . . . or was he thinking about Shelby?

"After my wife died, I had no intention of getting involved. With anyone. I just didn't have the time with my work and everything. Especially while parenting Lily. As you know, she can be a handful. But she comes first in my life."

"Of course." Madison tried to process this. This talk of dating, was it about Addie? Or her? Maybe he suspected both McDowell women had him in their sights.

"So I guess I'm not really sure how I feel. Does that even make sense?"

"Well, I can see how you have your hands full with Lily. She needs your attention. And there's the dirt bike project. That's going to take time. Plus, you have your consulting, and you've just started to build your home. There's a lot on your plate, Gavin. It's not surprising that you feel a little overwhelmed at the idea of . . . uh, dating."

"You got that right." He sounded relieved. "I just don't think I have time for a woman in my life. Not right now anyway."

"So maybe that's your answer. Maybe you should tell Addie that." Madison let out a relieved exhale over what seemed a simple solution to everything.

"I think you're right." He sat up straight, turning to look at her with a furrowed brow. "But I don't want to hurt her."

Madison bristled to imagine he did have feelings for her sister. "Because you might want to be involved with her someday and don't want to burn any bridges?"

"I don't really know . . . but it doesn't seem fair to string some-one along just to keep my options open. Does it?"

Madison grew even more irritated. She didn't appreciate being his sounding board when it came to his relationship with Addie. "I agree it doesn't seem fair," she said stiffly. "Well, unless the person wants to be strung along. And knowing Addie, she might not even care."

"Really?"

Madison stood, ready to escape what was turning unexpectedly painful. "Honestly, Gavin, I think this is a conversation you should be having with Addie. Not me."

He stood, reaching for her hand. "But I'm not good at this. You should know that as well as anyone."

What was that supposed to mean? Even more confused, she stepped back, but he was still grasping her hand. "Look, I know we've never talked about stuff . . . you know, our history, back when we were kids," she stammered. "But whatever it was that happened, I mean, when we were teens, is over and done. I want you to know I've left that all far behind me." Okay, that was a big fat lie. "And if you don't mind, I'd like to keep it that way." She tugged her hand from his. "Now, really, I need to get back to the party."

Gavin's brow was furrowed but he said nothing and, to her relief, remained behind at the bench. As Madison hurried off, returning to the warm, noisy barn, she felt flushed and flustered. What had he been attempting to tell her and why did it hurt so much? Had she totally misunderstood him? Had he misunderstood her?

As she crossed the crowded room, pretending to check on the cider supply, she felt Addie closely watching her. Was Addie upset by the two of them slipping out together earlier? Was she going to accuse her sister of going "after" him again? Did Madison even care?

"Hey, there you are. Just the gal I was looking for." Jeb Borden from Borden's Market grabbed her hand. "How 'bout a dance?"

She shrugged, then smiled. "Sure, why not?"

As she tried to keep up with the lively two-step, she noticed Gavin slip back in through the same side door she'd just used. Addie's eyes fixed upon him immediately. And she did not look happy. Poor Gavin looked out of place, perhaps as confused as Madison felt at the moment. What had actually transpired between them by the river? Would she ever figure it out?

12

The next week passed relatively quietly for Madison. Perhaps too quietly. She knew she should relish the downtime, especially after the frantic days of planting—not to mention that their busiest season was around the corner—but she still felt restlessly aggravated. It didn't help that Addie was giving her the silent treatment again, or that Gavin suddenly seemed to have vanished.

"He's just been super busy," Lily told her while helping to get the barn all set for wreath making, which would be starting soon. If it weren't for Lily's help and cheerful companionship, Madison would've been seriously lonely. But the girl, already in the habit of coming over, now made the Christmas tree farm her regular stop after doing some dirt bike runs after school.

"His consulting business?"

"I guess." Lily shrugged as she slid a ribbon bolt onto the pole by the cutting table. "He's always on his laptop. Or else he's walking around where the house is gonna be built and measuring things."

"How's that going?" Madison picked up a snared mess of florist wire.

"According to Dad, *slow*. But he's a major grouch about everything."

Madison wondered what was up, especially since it wasn't the first time Lily had referred to Gavin's foul mood, but she didn't plan to ask. "I thought I saw a concrete truck the other day so something must be happening."

"Yeah. The foundation's all done. You should come over and check it out. It's pretty cool. But it doesn't seem very big. Dad said that's an illusion and that it's bigger than I think, but I don't see how. I mean, it is what it is, right?"

Madison simply nodded but continued to untangle the wire. As curious as she was to see the building progress, she had no intention of checking it out.

"Yeah, I don't blame you for not wanting to come over since Dad's been Mr. Grumpy Pants."

Madison couldn't help but laugh.

"I think it might be thanks to Lucy."

Madison tried to remember—who was Lucy?

"She's gonna quit school again and Dad's pretty mad. At this rate, he thinks I'll finish college before she does."

Oh yeah, Gavin's oldest daughter. "What year is she?"

"I dunno." Lily shrugged. "Nobody does. Not even Lucy."

"Well, maybe she wants another kind of career path, you know, something that doesn't require a college degree."

"Dad says she just wants someone to take care of her." Lily spun around on the tall stool, sending her legs flying. "She should just find herself a rich guy and get married."

"Your dad wants her to do that?" Madison was disappointed.

"No, he doesn't *want* her to do that, but he thinks that's what *she* wants."

"Oh." Madison reached for the broom.

"Yeah, and now Lucy is having a hissy fit because Dad told her she can't come stay with us for winter break. Because, seriously, our trailer is *not* that big. I mean, can you imagine all three of us crammed in there like Vienna sausages in a can?" Lily laughed hard. "That's what I heard Dad tell her on the phone last night."

Madison felt a little sorry for Lucy. "Well, it might be hard on her, you know, not having a place to come home to for the holidays. I remember feeling like that a little. About going home to my mom's place because I wasn't that fond of my stepfather. But at least I could come here. This always felt more like home anyway."

"You have a stepdad?"

"Well, I did. But my mom finally divorced him."

"I don't think I'd like a stepmom." Lily hopped off the stool, then scampered to get the metal dustpan and held it while Madison swept in the dirt from the pine floor.

"But Lucy might really be feeling displaced." Madison watched Lily dump the dustpan into the trash. "It's too bad your new house isn't done."

"Yeah, that's what Dad keeps saying." She closed the metal garbage can with a loud bang. "But it is what it is."

"We have lots of room here," Madison said. "I'm sure Addie wouldn't mind having Lucy stay with us during the holidays."

"I'm sure Lucy would like that." Lily tilted her head with a furrowed brow. "But I might like it more. Then Lucy could stay with Dad." She chuckled. "It'd serve her right having to share that dinky bathroom and not have any closet space."

Madison grinned. "Might make her want to go back to college."

"Yeah. That'd make Dad happy." She twisted her mouth to one side. "But I think I'd miss being with Dad. He and I are buddies, ya know?"

Madison nodded. "I get that. Well, whichever works, why don't you tell your dad we have room here for one of you girls. As long as Addie is okay with it."

"Addie will probably love my sister. They like the same kinds of things." Lily rolled her eyes. "Fancy clothes and hair and shoes and stuff. You should've seen Lucy's closet when we lived at home. I had to pack it up to put in storage for her when we sold our house. Man, was she mad about that."

Suddenly Madison could picture this girl—just like her mother,

Shelby. Lily was probably spot-on right, Lucy and Addie would most likely get along just fine. Madison would be the odd one out. But it was too late to back out on her invitation.

"Do you need any more help?" Lily asked brightly.

Madison checked the time. "Nah, it'll be dark soon. I think we should call it a day. But thanks." She patted Lily on the back. "Besides being a good worker, you're great company. I appreciate it."

"Yeah, especially when Addie's snubbin' ya, huh?"

Madison felt her brows arch. So Lily had noticed. "Well, you know how it goes with sisters. You love 'em, but sometimes you want to strangle them, right?"

Lily laughed loudly as she opened the barn door. "Yep. Exactly."

The dusky November air felt cool and fresh on Madison's face as they walked out. "Think your dad's almanac is right? Think we'll get snow here this winter?"

"I hope so. It would be so pretty."

As usual, Madison walked Lily to the property line where she'd parked her dirt bike, watching as she tugged on her helmet, then they both waved goodbye. Thanks to an afternoon rain, there was no trail of dust as Lily rode back to their trailer. The lights from the trailer windows looked cheery with a friendly golden glow, but Madison wasn't so sure the occupant was feeling that friendly. At least, not toward her. Even though Lily was blaming other things for her dad's foul mood, Madison couldn't help but feel somewhat responsible, thanks to that awkward conversation by the river. She still couldn't quite remember how or why it had gone so sideways, but she suspected it was mostly her fault.

Seeing movement out of the corner of her eyes, she noticed Addie heading for the front porch and, feeling she had a good excuse for conversation, she called out, "Hey, Addie, got a minute?"

Addie paused with one hand on the front door. "Yeah, I guess. But it's cold out here."

Madison jogged up to the porch, following her sister into the warm front room. "I wanted to run something by you."

"What?" Addie scowled. "Have you decided to do something new with the tree farm? Maybe turn it into a B and B to make more money?"

Madison smiled. "Hey, you're getting warmer."

"Not seriously?" Addie's scowl deepened.

"No, not seriously." Madison explained about Lucy. "According to Lily, you'll like her. She has similar interests."

Addie looked skeptical. "What kind of similar interests?"

"She's into fashion and things like that."

"Oh?"

"And she won't have a place to stay during winter break. Not enough room in the camp trailer."

"Duh." Addie's brows arched. "Is Gavin on board with it?"

"I don't know. Lily plans to talk to him." Madison glanced away.

"You mean you don't plan to discuss it with him?" There was a very definite accusation in Addie's tone.

"What do you mean?" Madison looked directly at her.

"You know, like you did the night of the harvest party. Don't think I didn't see you sneaking off with him like that for a little tryst down by the river. I saw the whole thing."

Madison blinked. Had Addie been listening to their conversation?

"I should've known you'd try to steal him." Addie folded her arms in front of her.

"For your information, it was not like that at all." Madison stepped closer, locking eyes with her sister. "In fact, we were mostly talking about you."

Addie's brows shot up. "Me? Really?"

"Yes. Gavin wasn't sure what to do."

"What do you mean? What to do about what?"

"Well, he's not dense, Addie. He knows you were pursuing him. You're not exactly subtle."

"Yeah, okay. So what did he say?"

"Just that the whole dating thing was out of his comfort zone.

He didn't really know what to do about it." Madison thought that was pretty close to the truth.

"Seriously? So he really was trying to figure it out? And you were just helping him?"

"To be honest, I can't remember the whole conversation." Now that was the truth. "But yeah, he was trying to figure everything out."

"Oh, Madison." Addie hugged her. "I'm sorry. I did it again, didn't I? I misjudged my sister. And you were probably just looking out for me. I'm so sorry."

Madison didn't know what to say but returned the embrace. At least Addie would be talking to her now.

"So do you think Gavin wants to date?" Addie asked with hopeful eyes.

"I really don't know. Like he said, he's got a lot going on right now. Too many plates in the air. I think he might need some time."

Addie nodded. "Okay, I get that."

"Maybe the best we can do is be good neighbors and offer our friendship."

"Yeah, for sure. And his older daughter—what's her name, Lucy?—she can definitely stay with us. That actually sounds fun. In fact, I think we should just include their whole family in all our holiday plans. Don't you?"

Madison wasn't sure but mutely nodded.

"Won't it be fun filling this house with people? And, oh yeah, I forgot to tell you, Mom is coming too."

"Mom is coming here?" Madison mentally braced herself. It wasn't that she didn't love her mother, she definitely did. But when Addie and Mom were together, it always felt like two against one—with Madison always playing defense.

"Yeah, she'll come for Thanksgiving and maybe even stay through Christmas. She wants to help with the tree farm. She said she keeps reading more about the fires here and wants to do what she can to help us."

"Really?" Madison tried to wrap her head around the image of Mom in her beautiful designer clothes and expensive shoes out there in the mud and soot, helping cut down trees. "This I have to see."

Addie just laughed as she started up the stairs. "Hey, people can change, Madison. You just need to give 'em a chance."

"Right." Madison forced a smile. "Well, I won't turn away anyone who wants to help on the farm. Even if it's Mom. In fact, I promise to do whatever I can to make this the best Christmas ever. For Mom and everyone."

"I'll hold you to that promise. And *I* will decorate the whole house from top to bottom." Addie ran a hand over the old oak banister. "Just like Grandma used to. When it was just her and me, after Grandpa and Dad passed, well, we didn't do much. I think it's about time we did."

"I agree." Madison's smile felt genuine now. It warmed her heart to see her sister getting into a cheerful holiday spirit. Even if it did mean Mom would be here with all her fancy ideas and clueless suggestions. Madison remembered the year Mom had surprised Ray, as well as Addie and Madison, by decorating everything on their fake Christmas tree and throughout Ray's big fancy house in shades of blues and purples. Mom thought it was uptown and glamorous, but to Madison, it was just a blue, blue Christmas.

But that was a long time ago. Having her little family all together here on the farm might turn out to be fun. How long had it been since Madison had experienced an old-fashioned family Christmas? Just, please, she hoped there would be no blue decorations!

13

For the next couple of weeks, Madison occupied herself with getting everything set up for tree cutting. The youth group crew had showed up the weekend before, and Madison had supervised the whole thing. And now the preordered wholesale trees were all cut and wrapped and stacked alongside the driveway, but it would still be a couple days before they could be picked up. The goal was to have them out of there the day before Thanksgiving.

Madison was eager to see them gone. Oh, she knew the Christmas tree business was all about harvesting and selling trees—and hopefully making a profit—but seeing the tightly wrapped trees stacked in tall piles filled her with an unexpected sadness. Kind of like an evergreen graveyard. Of course, each one of these trees would be freed from its twined bondage and gloriously displayed on Christmas tree lots throughout the northwest. People would purchase them, and each one would eventually grace someone's home and hopefully fill the new owners with pine-scented Christmas joy.

As she pushed a wheelbarrow of mulch between a row of mature spruce trees in the U-cut section, she heard the sound of a dirt bike approaching. Suspecting it was Lily, though the engine noise sounded different than her usual bike, she paused to look.

"Hey, you," Lily called out. "Come here."

Madison smiled and waved, pushing the barrow toward the recently planted trees where she'd been mulching today. She waited for Lily to stop on the road that separated their properties. "What's up?"

Lily pointed to the machine beneath her. "My new bike arrived today."

"It's quieter than your old bike." Madison peeled off her gloves, shaking the mulch off.

"I thought you might like that. It's an e-bike."

"Nice!" Madison ran a finger over a shiny blue fender. "Good-looking too."

"Yeah, but it's not as powerful as my gas bike."

"Oh?"

"But that's okay. E-bikes are more *polite* for riding public trails. You know, where there are hikers or horses or dogs. Doesn't upset anyone. Dad got an e-bike too. So we can go on rides together. You know, off the property. Like along the river trail into town."

"What a great idea."

"Really?" Lily got a slightly sly look. "You think so?"

"Sure. A nice quiet ride down an interesting trail sounds fun."

"Great." Lily grinned. "Because I have something to show you."

"To show me?"

"Yeah. You busy right now?"

"Not really. I thought about making some more wreaths, but I think you and I got enough to keep us in business throughout the upcoming weekend."

"Yeah, they look so cool hanging on the barn." Lily pointed to the barrow. "What's that for?"

"Just taking it over to mulch the seedlings we planted."

"Wanna come over to our place for a minute? I want you to see something."

Madison shrugged. "I guess." Part of her wondered what was

going on, but the other part felt nervous. She hadn't really spoken to Gavin since the harvest party.

"Great. I'll meet ya there." And Lily took off.

Curiosity getting the best of her, Madison dumped the last of the mulch, then strolled over to the trailer. To be neighborly, she told herself as she approached the camping trailer and new outbuildings.

She spied Gavin emerging from their storage shed. He looked extra handsome in his denim coat and cowboy hat. "Hey, Madison." His expression was hard to read, but she sensed he felt as uncomfortable as she did just now.

"Hi there, Gavin." Madison shoved her hands in her jeans pockets as Lily disappeared into the storage shed. "Uh, Lily . . . said she wanted to show me something."

"Yeah. She's getting it." He came closer but kept his eyes on the shed. "There it is." He nodded toward Lily as she wheeled out a red bike. It looked very similar to the new blue one. Maybe a bit bigger.

"Another e-bike?" Madison tried to sound more interested than she felt. "Is that your new bike, Gavin? Pretty nice."

"Actually, it's *yours,*" he told her.

Madison's jaw dropped. "What?"

"It was Lily's idea." Gavin suddenly looked sheepish. "It's, um, our way of being good neighbors."

"No way." Madison felt her eyes growing wider.

"Yep." Lily rolled it over to her. "I picked red 'cause your Jeep is red. I thought you'd like that."

"I do like the color, but I—"

"We want you to enjoy riding as much as we do, Madison. Then maybe you'll see why we wanna make the dirt bike camp here." Lily's smile grew hopeful. "Don't you like it?"

Madison was speechless.

"And we want you to be safe." Gavin picked up a shiny red helmet that had been sitting on the picnic table. He looked slightly uneasy as he handed it to her.

"But I—I don't even know how to ride one of those things," Madison stammered.

"Do you know how to ride a regular bike?" Lily asked.

"Well, yeah, sure, but—"

"This is even easier," Lily assured her.

"But I've never been on anything like this. I mean, with a motor."

"That's okay." Lily grinned. "I'll teach you."

"But I can't just accept this. It's too much and I—"

"Come on, Madison," Lily pleaded. "You *have* to accept it. Just give it a try, *please*. I know you can do it. Trust me, you'll love it."

Gavin held up his hands, backing toward the trailer. "Okay, I'm going to step out of this. It's between you ladies now. I've got a Zoom meeting in a few minutes." He shot a nervous grin Madison's way. "Good luck."

Madison bit her lip, trying to think of a gentle way to reject Lily's unexpected generosity, but seeing the longing in the girl's eyes, she knew she couldn't. "Okay then . . . when's my first lesson?"

Lily clapped her hands together. "Now!" She pointed to Madison's work boots. "You've even got the right footwear." And just like that, Madison's first dirt bike lesson began. To Madison's surprise, Lily was a good teacher, going through each step on how to start the bike, control it, brake, and a few other tips. Before long, Madison was on the bike and moving—at a snail's pace—around and around the trail that Lily had been establishing on the perimeter of their property. She went a little faster each time until she began to get the hang of it. This really was easy. And it was fun!

"You're doing great," Lily told her when they finally paused for a break near the boundary between the two properties. "Do you *really* like it?"

Madison's smile widened. "I *really* do."

"I knew it!" Lily beamed at her as she unsnapped her helmet strap.

"But I still don't think I can keep this bike, Lily. It's too much to—"

"You have to keep it," she insisted. "We can't return it now. And I really want you to go riding with me. Especially when Dad's busy. We can take the river trail when you get more experienced."

Madison considered this. "That might be fun."

Lily pointed over to the Christmas tree property. "And just think how handy it can be. You can use it to get around over there. A bike's narrow enough to fit between the tree rows. Better than your ATV."

"You're probably right." Madison slowly nodded. "But I need to get better at steering first. Don't want to run down trees."

"We'll keep practicing," Lily told her. "Anytime you want."

"Okay. I don't really know what to say. I mean, I guess I should say thank you. Thank you very much, Lily. It's a very generous gift."

"You can thank Dad. I wanted it really bad, but he totally agreed."

"Well, please thank him for me." Madison noticed a silver car pulling down the long driveway toward her house. She recognized the Mercedes. "Uh-oh."

"Who's that?"

"My mother."

"Is that bad?" Lily squinted toward the sedan now parking in front of the house.

Madison shrugged. "Not really. I knew she was coming for Thanksgiving, but I didn't know she'd be here today. And my mom can be, well, difficult sometimes."

"So can my sister." Lily snickered. "And we have to pick her up tomorrow. And all her junk too."

"I thought she wasn't coming until winter break."

"Apparently Lucy already dropped out of college." Lily rolled her eyes. "Now she wants to come home. I mean, to stay here with you. Didn't Dad tell you?"

"Uh, no. But that's okay." Madison wondered if her new dirt

bike was some kind of thank-you for taking in Lucy. She watched as her mom emerged from her fancy car. As always, she was dressed impeccably. She tossed a long white scarf over her shoulder as the lid of her trunk opened.

"Man, I'm sure not looking forward to that long drive to Seattle." Lily sighed. "Stuck in the back seat since Lucy will probably take over the front. Plus, she'll have all her junk to pack in."

"Why don't you stay here on the farm with us?" Madison said absently.

"Seriously?" Lily's eyes lit up. "That'd be okay? I mean, it'll be overnight."

"Sure. Why not?" Madison started her bike's engine like an old pro.

"Thanks so much!" Lily beamed at her.

"I better go see about my mom." Madison settled into the seat and reached for the throttle. "Thanks again for the bike."

"Sure! And I'll give you another lesson after school tomorrow," Lily called as Madison carefully took off.

"See ya then," Madison called back. Concentrating on the things she'd just learned, Madison rode her new bike, perhaps a bit too quickly, over to the front porch.

"My goodness." Mom looked shocked. "What in the world are you doing on that thing?"

Madison turned off the engine and removed her helmet. "Hi, Mom."

"I didn't know my daughter was a motorcycle mama."

Madison forced a smile. "It's not a motorcycle, Mom."

"It's got a motor and wheels." Her mom paused next to the open trunk.

"It's an e-bike."

"An e-bike? How utterly charming." Mom's voice seeped with sarcasm. "Why on earth are you riding it?" She struggled to tug out a large Louis Vuitton suitcase, then dropped it to the ground like a load of bricks.

"Let me get that." Madison was tempted to give her mom a welcome hug, but they'd never really been a huggy sort of family. Instead, she moved the large suitcase out of the way, then extracted a slightly smaller one from the trunk.

"I can get this." Mom pulled a small, third matching bag out.

"Welcome to the farm," Madison said as they went up the steps. "I didn't think you were coming until Wednesday."

"Didn't Addie tell you I called yesterday?"

"No, but I was pretty busy with tree cutting." She wasn't about to mention that she and her baby sister were still barely talking. Let Mom figure a few things out for herself.

"I saw all those tree piles along the road. Did you cut them all yourself?"

Madison laughed. "Hardly. But I supervised." She set a case down to open the door. "I wish I'd known you were coming sooner. We might've coordinated your trip with our neighbor's daughter. She's been in school up your way. She'll be staying with us too."

"Oh? A full house?"

"It's a big house, Mom. And if Addie knew you were coming, I'm sure she got the master bedroom all set. She mentioned moving back to her old bedroom upstairs while you're here."

"Well, I don't want to put anyone out."

"No one's put out, Mom." Madison waited for her mother to go inside, where Addie was running down the stairs and, although they'd never been openly affectionate, she embraced her mother. Madison stared at them, wondering how and when these changes came about.

"I'm so glad to see you, Mom. Did you have a good trip?" Addie picked up her smallest bag.

"Traffic was awful. I thought I'd avoid some of that by coming earlier, but it seems everyone and their aunt Martha is on the road today."

"Well, I'm so glad you're here. You get Grandma and Grandpa's room." Addie linked arms with her, leading Mom down the hall. "I cleaned it really nice for you." Madison followed with the two larger bags.

"I know it's not what you're used to," Addie said, setting the bag on a bench by the bed, "but it's the best we have. And the bathroom is just a door down. Madison and I can use the upstairs bath while you're here."

"And your other guest?" Mom sat on the edge of the bed. "Where will she stay?"

"The spare room upstairs."

"And all three of you will share that little bathroom up there?" Mom frowned. "Cozy."

"Well, if it gets too cozy, I might use the downstairs bath with you." Addie smiled. "You don't mind, do you?"

Mom chuckled. "Like old times."

"I've got soup in the Crock-Pot," Madison said. "I better check on it."

"You cook now?" Mom sounded surprised.

"It's nothing new. Grandma taught me a few tricks when I was a kid. Then I had to cook a lot in Mongolia. No easy fast food there."

"Yes, Madison is quite the little culinary queen." Addie smirked. "Although our tastes differ some."

Madison resisted an eye roll as she moved toward the door. "Well, it's just veggie and rice soup, if anyone's interested. And I could make some muffins."

"Or you can come out with me, Mom," Addie eagerly suggested. "It's about a twenty-minute drive to some good restaurants but well worth the drive."

"Do you mind, Madison?" Mom's finely plucked brows arched.

"Not at all. Do as you like. I always make a big pot of soup just to have leftovers the next couple days." Madison tried to appear casual but had mixed feelings as she headed for the kitchen. If she had known she was dining alone, she would've added chicken to the soup! Sure, she was relieved to escape their chitchat reunion, but she felt left out too. *Better get used to it,* she thought as she peeled off her hoodie to hang by the door. It was a good thing she had plenty to keep her busy between now and Christmas. The barn could probably use a few more wreaths.

14

The weather turned nasty just as the last of the trees were getting cut and wrapped and picked up. Torrential rains had turned the farm into a mudfest. But the teens from the youth organization were finally done loading the last truck. Madison waved to the driver, then turned to Lily, who'd been her right-hand gal these past couple of weeks.

"Thanks for all your help today." She patted Lily's soggy shoulder. "You're soaked."

"So are you."

"Let's get into some dry clothes." As Madison turned toward the house, her phone pinged. She extracted it from her pocket to see a text from Gavin. "Your dad says they're almost here."

"I guess I need to move my stuff back to the trailer," Lily said glumly as they stomped their muddy feet on the back porch.

"Yeah, Lucy will need the room you're in now. Unless you two want to bunk together." Madison studied Lily.

"No way, José." Lily scowled.

"Well, I'm sure your dad will appreciate your company."

Lily brightened. "Yeah, you're right."

"But you can grab a hot shower and get into dry clothes first." She led the way into the warm house where Addie and Mom were studying a cookbook and arguing about turkeys. Since Madison had been busy with the trees, her mom and sister had taken over the kitchen. And neither was a particularly gifted cook.

"You're getting mud all over the kitchen," Addie scolded. "Can't you take those wet things off on the porch?"

"Sorry." Madison backed her and Lily out the door. "Never mind if we catch pneumonia," she muttered.

"Or hypothermia," Lily added.

As they peeled off their soggy clothes and muddy boots, Madison wondered what her mom and sister were conjuring up for dinner tonight, or were they too distracted with preparations for tomorrow? So far their combined culinary skills had been disappointing. Not that she was complaining.

"I'm starved." Lily draped her jacket over an old wicker chair.

"Me too."

"I hope Addie doesn't make vegetarian meatloaf again."

Madison laughed. "The fact she couldn't get anyone to eat her leftovers should've been a clue."

"Maybe you should cook tonight," Lily suggested.

"I wish I could take over, but Addie and my mom have commandeered the kitchen."

"Looks like they're still holding out for Thanksgiving too."

"Unfortunately." Madison sighed. Last night she'd tried to talk sense into Addie, but it was pointless. Addie was convinced that she could impress Gavin by putting together the perfect holiday meal.

"Tofu turkey?" Lily teased.

"Thank goodness, no. My mom already bought a fresh turkey."

"Hopefully they won't ruin that."

"Let's get inside." Madison opened the door, trying to get Lily past the "cooks," who were still disputing the best way to cook the turkey the next day. Mom insisted the best turkeys were cooked slowly on low heat, and Addie was certain it should be roasted hot and fast on high. Apparently they found evidence to support both theories.

"Wait a minute." Mom grabbed Madison's arm. "You're a good cook. What do you think?"

"I, uh, I've never cooked a whole turkey before." Madison tipped her head to Lily to keep going.

"Neither has Addie, but she has an opinion," Mom told her.

"Mom wants to cook the turkey all night and all day on super low heat," Addie told Madison.

"My best friend Beth Greenburg cooks her turkeys like that, and they're juicy and tender and amazing," Mom declared.

"Sounds like a formula for food poisoning to me," Addie complained.

Mom still held Madison's arm. "What do you think?"

"Well, I do remember Mongolians cooking their pork really slowly, like for hours and hours. It was always really good, and no one died."

"Then it's settled," Mom said. "Low and slow."

Addie glared at Madison as if she were personally to blame for their troubles.

Madison just shrugged. "Not to change the subject, but"—she glanced around the kitchen where various Thanksgiving ingredients were piled here and there—"do we have any plans for dinner?"

"You mean for tonight?" Mom turned to Addie. "I need to get the turkey into the oven and prepare some things for tomorrow. You want to handle dinner?"

Addie pursed her lips. "Well, I'm not really hungry. I'd be fine with some yogurt and fruit."

"Lily and I are starving. So if you don't mind, I'll fix dinner tonight."

"Suit yourself." Addie sounded nonchalant.

"I will." As Madison hurried to get into some dry clothes, she decided to make a big pot of spaghetti and meat sauce, as well as a smaller pot of veggie sauce in case Addie chose to join them. That would be relatively easy and provide her and Lily with a hearty meal. Plus, if Gavin and Lucy arrived hungry at dinnertime, she'd have enough to share.

By the time Madison was clean and dry, Mom was just finishing up her pre-Thanksgiving preparations, which, in Madison's opinion, didn't appear to be much, but she didn't plan to mention it. Comparing Mom to her grandmother had blown up in her face enough times for her to know it was a big mistake. Still, she couldn't help but mentally contrast the way Grandma would have been baking pies all day compared to picking up the store-bought pumpkin and apple pies that now sat on the counter. And they had Cool Whip to go on top. She saw it while grabbing French bread from the freezer. No whipping of cream tomorrow.

Madison noticed cans of green beans, soup, and French fried onions lined up for green bean casserole as she sautéed the ground beef, onions, and garlic for her meat sauce. She wondered if she should inform Mom of the mason jars of green beans in the pantry—ones Grandma had grown and put up last summer. Maybe it was best not to rock the boat. She didn't want to douse Mom's enthusiasm over cooking their feast.

As she removed veggies from the fridge, she grimaced at the lime gelatin salad—Mom's "specialty" and something Madison suspected no one else would touch. Oh, well. She decided to just be grateful to have the day off tomorrow.

"Smells yummy." Lily leaned over to see what Madison was stirring. "Need any help?"

"Want to chop some veggies?" Madison nodded to the produce by the sink.

"Sure." Lily got busy, and the two of them worked quietly together.

"Feels good to be in a warm kitchen," Madison said as she set a pot of water on the stove.

"Yeah. And it's fun to fix dinner in a regular-sized kitchen. So much better than the trailer."

"I'll bet that's a challenge."

"Yeah. It was better in the summer when we could grill stuff outside. But Dad's talking about making a covered outdoor kitchen where they're building our house."

"That's a great idea."

"Speaking of great ideas, I was thinking about wreaths at school today."

Madison laughed. "Daydreaming about wreaths in math class?"

"Something like that." Lily smirked at her. "I was thinking about ways we could make them different. Like maybe use action figures on some. Or like little model cars? Ya know? Like, my dad really loves Cobra cars, and I got him a little red one for his birthday last summer. Wouldn't something like that look cool on a wreath?"

"Custom wreaths?" Madison considered this. "That's pretty clever."

"Yeah. I thought so."

"Maybe we can experiment with that next week. After the U-cutters this weekend, we should be in need of more wreaths."

"I still get to help, right?"

"Of course, I'm counting on you." Madison patted her back. "You're my right-hand girl."

The pasta water was just starting to boil when Madison heard voices in the living room. "Sounds like someone's here." She peeked out the steamy kitchen window. "Looks like your dad's SUV out there. Wanna go see if they've had dinner yet?"

Lily came back after a few minutes. "Dad says they haven't eaten since a pretty lousy lunch on the road. Addie's showing Lucy the room right now. She'll probably complain that I didn't change the sheets."

"Can't Lucy do that?" Madison checked the toaster oven to see that the loaf was just starting to turn golden.

"Hard to say." Lily snickered. "She can be kinda helpless. Want me to set the table?"

"Thank you! And I'll take over the veggies. Tell everyone we're about twenty minutes out."

Lily left and Madison hummed contentedly to herself as she bustled about the kitchen, chopping more veggies for a salad and draining the pasta. She was just pouring the sauce over the spaghetti when she heard a loud clunk behind her. She whipped around to see Gavin, still in his jacket, setting a large fruit basket and what looked like a pastry box on the kitchen table.

"Didn't mean to startle you." His smile was warm. "I was just enjoying this homey scene. Most welcome after driving through that rainstorm all day long."

"Thats okay." She pushed a loose strand of hair from her face and returned his smile. "Dinner's almost ready. It's kind of just thrown together. But Lily and I were ravenous after working outside all day."

"Looks like all the trees got picked up." He removed his jacket, gave it a shake, then hung it on a peg by the back door. "Did that go okay?"

"Other than the rain and mud, it was fine. And all that moisture should help keep the trees fresh and green that much longer. Thank you for the lovely fruit basket." She tapped the white box. "What's in here?"

"Cinnamon rolls from my favorite bakery in Seattle. Thought you ladies might enjoy them tomorrow morning." He removed a bottle of wine from the basket.

"Well, you're very thoughtful."

"I have some rolls in the car for Lily and me too. It's a small token of my appreciation for your help with my girls." With the wine bottle in one hand, he opened the utensil drawer. "Mind if I uncork this?"

"Not at all."

Before long, he'd poured a bit of red wine into a pair of wine-glasses. "Why don't you sample it to be sure it's compatible with whatever you're cooking?" He handed her a glass. "What *are* you cooking?"

"Just spaghetti with meat sauce."

"Smells delicious." He held up his glass and was just clinking hers when Addie stepped into the kitchen. "Here's to the cook," he said.

"Excuse me." Addie's tone was slightly sharp. "I hope I'm not interrupting anything."

"Cheers." Madison held up her glass toward Addie, then took a sip.

"Lucy needs you to unlock the car so she can bring in the rest of her bags," Addie told Gavin.

"Tell her I'll unload them for her after dinner. Maybe the deluge will calm down some by then." He crossed to the cupboard and got down another wineglass. "Care to join us, Addie?"

"Sure." She seemed to warm a bit as he handed her a glass.

"I was just expressing my gratitude to Madison for helping with my girls. Thank you, too, Addie. I have the best neighbors ever."

Madison could hear Mom calling from the other room now.

"That's my mom," Addie told Gavin. "Have you ever met her?"

"Maybe . . . a long time ago. But I don't really remember."

"Well, come meet her again." Addie tugged him by the arm. "And bring that bottle with you." Just like that, Madison had the kitchen all to herself again. She didn't really mind as she scurried around putting the finishing touches on dinner. Although she had no doubts about what Addie was up to. Gavin was still her territory—and she wanted Madison to know it!

15

Madison woke to the aroma of roasting turkey the next morning. Thinking her mom and sister had today's meal under control, she went outside to do some chores. She filled her wheelbarrow with dropped fir and spruce branches, then took the greens over to the barn for more wreath and garland making next week. After the rush.

She knew tomorrow and throughout the weekend would be super busy for the tree farm. Families still full of turkey and holiday goodwill would come out here to merrily cut a tree. She still remembered Grandma saying how November was too early to put up a Christmas tree, but she'd done her part to make sure U-cutters went home happy, just the same. While her ancient stereo played Christmas music on old LP records, she'd serve cocoa and hot cider and cookies and sell garlands and wreaths.

After emptying her load of greens, she noticed her shiny red dirt bike plugged in to its charger in the barn. It was still a little muddy out, but Lily had been saying how that made riding even more fun, and Madison wondered, *Why not?* She tugged her helmet on and was soon sporting around the property.

She spied Lily doing the same thing over on their land and decided to join her. Lily was on her noisier gas-powered bike but took some time to give Madison a few tips for riding on more slippery ground. Then they were off, sliding a little here and there but not too fast and nothing too daring. They finally stopped by the camp trailer where Gavin had a nice bonfire going with an old-fashioned metal coffeepot steaming on a grate.

"Coffee?" He held up a cup.

She tugged off her helmet. "I'd love some."

"You gals are a muddy mess," he teased as he filled a mug.

"I noticed." Madison attempted to brush mud splats from her jeans.

Lily still straddled her bike. "That's part of the fun," she said. "And now that Miss Poky Pants is taking a break, I'm really going to cut loose and go for it."

"Thanks a lot, Speedy Pants," Madison said sarcastically.

"Be safe," Gavin called as she revved her motor and took off.

"She will be, won't she?" Madison asked.

"Of course. Lily understands the rules. If she's not safe, she loses riding privileges. Not to mention she might wind up in pain."

"You're pretty nonchalant about that."

"Remember all the crazy things we did as kids?"

She felt her cheeks warm as she sat in the camp chair he'd pulled out for her. There were some things she didn't care to remember.

"Anyway, I like to give Lily freedom where I can. I think it helps her be more responsible. I sometimes wonder if Lucy would be doing better if we'd been more like that with her. We were so young. Like kids raising kids. And Shelby was so overprotective. Well, I wonder if Lucy got a little spoiled." He paused to sip his coffee. "How's she doing over there anyway?"

"Okay, I guess. She and Addie and Mom seemed to hit it off. They stayed up late last night. After I went to bed, I could hear their movie playing and them talking. And everyone was quiet this morning. Although the whole house smells like roasting turkey, so I assume the food's all under control."

Gavin reached for a pastry box very similar to the one he'd brought them last night. "Tried these yet?"

"I totally forgot about those when I snuck out earlier."

He popped open the lid, revealing decadent goodies. "Care for one?"

"Thanks." She picked up a gooey pastry.

"With caramel, cinnamon, pecans, raisins, they're highly addictive."

"And yummy," she said as she chewed her first bite.

"Your mom said Thanksgiving dinner would be around two." He set down the box. "I have to say I'm looking forward to it. We haven't done much of anything for any holidays the past couple of years. No one's seemed to really care."

"I'm sure it must be hard starting new traditions."

"Yeah." He nodded. "But it's time. I feel like we've entered a new era, Madison." He smiled. "And I love that you're my neighbor. It's like having family again."

She returned his smile. "It is like family, isn't it? I've really enjoyed Lily's company. By the way, if you don't mind, I'd love to have her help—I mean, as much as she wants—throughout the pre-Christmas season."

"Oh, she *wants*. Just this morning, she was telling me about all these wacky wreath ideas she's got. I'm not sure they're good ideas, but she thinks there are wreaths for everyone's different taste."

"A regular entrepreneur."

"I guess." He gazed out to where Lily was coming down the biggest hill they'd made, her bike slipping to the right and the left but staying the course. "She's a really good rider."

"And a good teacher too."

He turned back to her. "I noticed you're getting more confident."

"I'm actually loving it."

"Loving it?"

"Yes. It's freeing and fun. And sometimes it makes for a great little escape." She almost said "from Addie," but stopped herself.

"What could you possibly have to escape from?" His eyes twinkled as he tipped his head toward the tree farm.

She shrugged, then took another gooey bite.

"I mean, there's Addie and your mom and my slightly entitled daughter over there." He laughed. "Honestly, those three at dinner last night. I swear it was like three peas in a pod."

She couldn't help but laugh too.

"City girls. All three of them."

She nodded eagerly. "You got that right."

Now his expression turned serious. "Shelby was like that too."

She wasn't sure how to respond. "I didn't really know her very well, Gavin. I mean, she seemed nice. And she was really pretty. But . . ." Her voice trailed.

"Not exactly my type?" he finished for her.

"I guess I wondered."

"Everyone did." He sighed.

Lily was zipping back toward them now, her tires spitting mud before she stopped by the fire. "That was awesome!" She pulled her helmet off. "Any more of those rolls left, Dad?"

"I saved the last one for you." He handed her the box.

"Good thing too," Madison teased. "I might've been tempted to take it."

"Want half?" Lily offered. "I already had two."

"No thanks." Madison stood. "If I'm lucky, there might still be some at home. And speaking of home, I should probably get back to see if they need a hand with dinner today."

"Knowing their cooking abilities, I'm sure they will," Lily said, making her dad laugh.

"Yeah, I was glad you were the cook last night," Gavin told Madison as she fastened her helmet strap.

"I should warn you not to get your hopes up too much for today," she said. "It'll probably be fine, but I know it won't be anything like what my grandma used to make. I'm going to put dibs on cooking dinner for Christmas."

"I second the motion." Gavin stood. "Thanks for joining my campfire this morning. Stop by anytime."

She promised she would. As she got on her bike, she considered how things were improving between her and Gavin, although she was not completely sure why. She waved goodbye and then made a slightly slippery but not embarrassing exit.

Back at the house, no one seemed to have missed her. Mom and Addie were in the kitchen, so to avoid being scolded for tracking in mud, she removed her boots on the front porch before slipping into the front room. She paused to admire the beautiful dining table. They'd set six places with Grandma's best china and silver on a handsome linen tablecloth with lovely fall-colored floral arrangements and candles ready to light. Perfection, and much better than she would've done.

Satisfied that all was under control, she tiptoed upstairs, unbeknownst to anyone. Then, deciding to enjoy the leisurely moment, as well as an unoccupied bathroom, she took a long shower and even unbraided and washed her hair. Something she'd been neglecting to do with the busyness of late. Back in her room, she took more time than usual to look nice. After all, it was a holiday. She could get grubby again tomorrow.

Then she sat down with a book she'd been meaning to start and read until one o'clock. Feeling a bit guilty, she went down to offer her help. Although the kitchen looked slightly chaotic, her mom and sister assured her things were under control and, seeing the sun shining outside, Madison decided to take a peaceful little stroll. She was curious about Lucy's whereabouts and considered inviting her to come along, but based on what she'd discovered about the young woman the night before, she assumed Lucy wasn't exactly a nature lover.

By two o'clock, she was really hungry. But when she went into the house, it didn't appear that dinner was ready. Gavin and his girls were sitting in front of a football game in Grandpa's den with a plate of not very appetizing appetizers in front of them.

She greeted them and sat down. "Who's playing?"

Gavin and Lily gave her the lowdown while Lucy, hunched over with her nose in her phone, ignored her entirely.

"These any good?" She picked up a cracker with something pink and green on it and gave it a sniff.

"It's salmon spread with kippers," Gavin told her.

"That sounds okay to me." She took a bite. "Not bad."

"If you like fish," Lucy said in a snarky tone.

Madison was just taking a second cracker when she heard Mom calling them to dinner. Soon all six were seated at the table, which now had the traditional dishes and a golden turkey ready and waiting. Gavin said a Thanksgiving prayer and, at Mom's request, began to carve the turkey.

"It smells delicious," he said. "And looks very moist." He sliced generous pieces, putting them onto the plates as Addie handed them to him.

Madison pretended to enjoy the potatoes that tasted like instant ones, and the dressing that she knew came from a box, as well as gravy that was too salty. She noted that Addie was eating some turkey substitute, and suddenly Madison felt uneasy about the turkey on her own plate. What if it hadn't been properly cooked? Yet everyone but Addie seemed to be enjoying it. Besides, what could she do without offending her mother? Mom seemed entirely pleased with herself, playing the perfect hostess and enjoying center stage.

Madison just wanted to get through this meal as graciously as possible. She suspected they all did. As they were finishing up, Gavin suggested they all share things they were thankful for. After a bit of balking, they all chimed in.

"I'm thankful I get to have my dirt bike park," Lily proclaimed. "I can't wait till we're open with lots of kids and campers."

"And I'm thankful to be home again after so long," Madison added.

Addie set her napkin on her plate. "I'm glad just to have friends and family around for a change."

"I'm thankful to be with my two girls for the holidays." Mom beamed at her daughters. "The first time in years."

"And I'm grateful for such wonderful neighbors," Gavin told them. "It's like having a bigger family."

"We're glad to be your family," Addie said.

Next Mom suggested they wait and have dessert and coffee in the front room a little later. In the meantime, Madison offered to clear and clean up. Her family members did not protest this.

"I'll help," Lily offered.

"Me too." Gavin began to collect plates.

"No, you're our guests," Addie insisted. "Guests aren't allowed to help."

Gavin pouted. "And here you were treating us like family."

"That's right," Madison pointed out. "If he wants to help, let him."

"It'll feel good to move around after such a heavy meal," he told them.

So Gavin, Lily, and Madison became KP, quickly discovering their work was cut out for them. After about an hour, they were nearly done, but Lily had suddenly grown very quiet. When Madison looked at the girl more closely, she seemed oddly pale.

"Are you okay?" Madison asked.

Lily shook her head. "I don't feel so good." She looked at Gavin. "My stomach hurts. I wanna go home, Dad."

"Sure, honey. We can go." He glanced nervously at Madison.

"Do you think it was something she ate?" Madison whispered to him.

He looked uneasy. "My stomach's starting to rumble a little too."

Madison winced. "I'll get your coats."

Before long, Gavin and Lily had exited through the kitchen door. Curious as to how the others were feeling, Madison went to tell them. Mom, Addie, and Lucy were visiting in the front room and seemed to feel perfectly fine, so Madison downplayed the tummy troubles. But it wasn't long until she felt sick too.

Before the day was over, everyone but Addie was sick. By now they knew, thanks to Addie's googling, it had to be from the turkey not reaching the proper temperature while cooking. Fortunately, it wasn't life-threatening. And Madison was grateful that her case appeared to be lighter than Mom's or Lucy's. But it was no fun. It wasn't until late that night that Madison finally felt better and realized she should check in on Gavin and Lily.

"Lily seems to have it worse than me," Gavin said in a hushed tone. "Although mine was bad enough. But I finally got her to keep down some chocolate milk, and she's sleeping now."

"I'm so sorry," she told him.

"It wasn't your fault."

"My mom's very sorry too."

"How's Lucy faring?"

"Let's just say she's not a real happy camper."

"Yes, I can imagine."

"But I do think everyone's feeling better. The worst must be over with. And I have to give Addie credit. She's trying to be a good nurse. Taking soda crackers and drinks to everyone. Of course, she keeps reminding us how this never would've happened if we'd only listened to her. Or if we'd all become vegetarians."

"I have to admit that's suddenly appealing."

She tried to laugh, but it sounded hollow. "I hope you both feel much better tomorrow."

"You too. I know you have a busy day ahead. And Lily's been fretting she won't be able to help now."

"Tell her not to worry. Just get better."

"Maybe Addie can step up since she didn't get hit with this."

"Yeah. Maybe." Even so, Madison doubted it. Addie had zero interest in the tree farm these days. It was almost as if she wanted it to fail. In fact, if she'd been the one cooking the turkey, Madison might've suspected sabotage. But she knew it was just a silly mistake. Even more glad she'd barely touched the turkey on her plate, she prayed they'd all get well quickly and that she'd have the strength she needed to make it through tomorrow.

16

Madison still didn't feel on top of her game the next morning. She managed to rise early enough to get things ready for the U-cutters that she expected to show up at nine, but she was moving uncharacteristically slow. She'd briefly considered putting up a sign by the road saying they were closed for the day, but she'd run ads since last week with a big festive promotion for today. She knew how families would make a special effort to get their trees and might even drive a long way—she hated to disappoint them.

As she spread a Christmassy tablecloth over the picnic table and set up things for cocoa, cider, and coffee, she was thankful that at least the weather was cooperating. The air was cool and crisp and should've felt refreshing. Instead, it made her shiver.

She returned to the house to grab a warmer coat and the packaged cookies she'd bought earlier in the week. They weren't homemade like the ones Grandma used to serve, but hopefully no one would care. As she opened the packages and filled the red-and-green basket with cookies, she realized that the house was still very quiet. Normally, that wouldn't concern her since she knew her housemates weren't early risers, but because of yesterday's turkey trouble, she wondered if she should check on their welfare. Or maybe ask Addie to . . .

She went upstairs and tapped on her sister's door.

"What is it?" a groggy voice answered. "What d'ya want?"

Madison cracked open the door. "Addie," she whispered, "I'm setting up for the U-cutters outside. Can you check on Mom and Lucy and make sure they're okay?"

Addie groaned and rolled over.

"I've kinda got my hands full today," Madison pressed. "A little help would be—"

"Fine. Yes. I'll check on them." Addie sat up, glaring at Madison. "Just go sell your stupid trees, okay?"

"Okay." Madison backed up, quietly closing the door. So much for sisterly help! Suppressing frustration, she went back outside to set things up as best as she could with her throbbing headache. She longed to feel some Christmas cheerfulness and wanted to enjoy the celebration of their opening day, but it took all her strength to just keep shuffling one foot in front of the other. Even the sound of cheery Christmas music coming through the speakers in the barn was aggravating to her head. But as cars and pickups began to pull up the driveway, she forced herself to smile and welcome their guests.

For the first couple of hours, Madison mechanically put herself through the paces, showing customers where the saws and garden carts were located, pointing out the balls of twine for securing trees to car tops, inviting them to partake in refreshments, and even selling a number of wreaths and garlands. But by noon, she felt drained, completely exhausted, and still had a pounding head. Tired of sweet cider and cocoa, she ducked into the house for a glass of grapefruit juice and literally bumped into her sister as she emerged from the kitchen.

"Hey, watch it," Addie told her, balancing a mug in her hand.

"Sorry," Madison stammered. "Thirsty. Need juice." She clutched the doorframe to steady herself.

Addie put her hand on Madison's shoulder, peering curiously at her. "Are you okay?"

"Just tired. Thirsty. Headache."

Addie escorted Madison into the kitchen and, after sitting her down at the little table, poured a glass of juice. "Here, drink this."

Madison sipped on the cold liquid.

Addie gave her an aspirin. "Take this." Next, she handed her a peeled banana. "And eat this. All of it. You probably need potassium."

"But the U-cutters." She took a bite of banana and chewed. "I need to get back out."

"Not right now." Addie watched until Madison finished her banana, then she helped her to stand. "Mom and Lucy both feel pretty rotten too. But they're keeping down fluids better today. I've been checking on them."

"Good. They got it worse. I mean, they're sicker than me. I didn't eat much turkey." Madison felt bone-tired as Addie led her through the living room.

"I want you to take a break." Addie gently pushed her down to the couch. "I'll cover for you outside."

"Really?" Madison was too exhausted to protest.

"Really." Addie tossed an afghan over Madison's legs. "Just rest. Okay?"

"Okay." Madison leaned back and closed her eyes. "Thanks, Addie."

• ● •

It was late afternoon by the time Madison woke up. She felt remarkably better but was shocked to see it was after three. She got herself a drink of water in the kitchen, where Mom and Lucy, looking pale in their nightclothes, were seated at the table with mugs of tea. She exchanged a quick greeting, then hurried outside to check on the U-cut situation. Hopefully Addie was still helping their customers.

"Hey there." Addie looked up from straightening the refreshment table. "You look a little more alive now."

"I feel more alive." Madison noticed several vehicles still parked along the driveway. "How's business?"

"It's been super busy." Addie actually looked pleased. "I don't know how all the other years went as far as U-cut tree sales, but I suspect we've had a record day." She pointed to the barn. "And look, I've sold most of your wreaths too."

"Wow. Guess I'll need to make more."

"Someone told me we're supposed to close up at four. Is that right?"

"That's what I put in the ad. Nine to four. Since it's getting dark by then."

"Good. I'm ready to call it a day."

"I can take it from here," Madison told her. "If you need to go inside."

Addie glanced toward the house. "How are Mom and Lucy?"

Madison described what she'd just witnessed, and Addie decided to remain outside until closing time. "It's been kinda fun helping out here."

Madison was surprised. "Thanks, Addie. For everything. Your help today really means a lot to me."

Addie just shrugged. "Hey, isn't that what sisters are for?"

Madison smiled. "I'd like to think so." She spotted a couple of families coming up to pay for trees and get refreshments, so both the sisters got busy. Finally, the last pickup, packed with three trees and two wreaths, was on its way, and Madison rode her dirt bike down the road to put the Closed sign up.

On her way back, she felt even more alive with the cool air on her face and realized she really was on the mend. But concern for Lily led her to ride over and check on her neighbors.

"She slept most of the day," Gavin quietly told her out in front of the trailer. "I'm planning to coax some chicken noodle soup into her. I had some myself and feel a lot better now."

"That's a great idea." She told him about her day with the U-cutters and how much Addie had helped. "I was pleasantly surprised."

"See how good things can come out of bad? If you hadn't been sick, Addie might not have stepped in." He rubbed his beard. "You're such a strong person, Madison. Maybe God has to knock you down a few notches to remind you that you need others."

Madison considered this. "Interesting theory. I guess being under the weather did give Addie the opportunity to play the hero. She probably enjoyed that."

Gavin grinned as he gently punched her in the arm. "It's okay to let people help you."

She nodded but knew he was talking about more than just Addie. "Well, thinking about chicken soup actually makes me a tiny bit hungry. I guess I'll go home and heat up a can or two. Maybe I can get Mom and Lucy to have some too."

"Why not let Addie handle that for you?" His eyes twinkled like this was a challenge. "I'm sure she can manage something that simple. Might help her self-esteem."

"Maybe so." She pulled her helmet back on. "I'll keep that in mind." As she slowly rode home, she knew he was probably right about letting Addie help her more, but at the same time, something about that bothered her. Why was Gavin suddenly feeling so protective of Addie? Maybe he was more interested in Addie than he'd let on. And if so, maybe it was time for Madison to get over herself.

17

That evening, Madison slipped out to the barn to start putting together a few more wreaths to hang out on the barn the next day. She wasn't worried about losing sales so much as disappointing anyone who hoped to take a wreath home with them. Besides that, it just felt good being out in the barn. She'd brought out a mug of herbal tea and put some calm Christmas music on the stereo. The peace and quiet seemed preferable to being cooped up in the house with the three city girls, all who were feeling much better after consuming chicken soup, compliments of Addie, who was a wiz at opening cans and nuking bowls in the microwave. Gavin was probably right about self-esteem issues.

"Hello in there?" called a female voice from the barn door.

"Hi there," Madison answered.

"We wondered what happened to you." Addie came over to the workbench and watched as Madison wired a clump of holly onto the wreath she was constructing.

"Sorry. I should've mentioned I was coming out here."

Addie pulled up a stool and leaned her elbows on the table. "So, do you really like doing this? Or are you just a glutton for punishment?"

"Punishment?" Madison blinked. "I *love* doing this. I always looked forward to wreath time at Thanksgiving."

"You and Grandma." Addie shook her head.

"Lily likes it too." Madison twisted the wire. "By the way, she and Gavin are both feeling much better tonight."

"Did he call you?" Addie sounded overly interested.

"Actually, Lily called." Madison knew better than to mention she'd spoken to Gavin personally this afternoon. "Lily wanted to be sure she could come help tomorrow."

"Oh, so you won't need me then?"

Madison looked up. "I didn't say that. It was really great having your help today, Addie. I never could've done it without you. You were a true godsend."

"Thanks. But, really, selling trees has never been my cup of tea."

"That's okay." Madison nodded toward a roll of plaid ribbon by Addie's elbow. "Can you hand me that?"

Addie gave it to her, then watched as Madison unfurled a length, rolling it into a circle she would fashion into a bow. She gathered the loops into place, squeezed them tightly in the middle, wrapped the wire around, then fluffed it out. "Voila."

"You're good at that," Addie observed.

"Grandma taught me everything I know."

"I always hated the whole wreath-making business. My fingers would get pricked by holly, and my nails would get dirty and broken. Plus, I just wasn't any good at it. The whole thing just felt torturous to me."

"Then be glad no one is asking you to help."

"But I suppose I could learn how."

"Seriously?" Madison secured the bow to the wreath and held it up to scrutinize.

"Look, Madison. I know I've been a wet blanket about the tree farm. I guess I just gave up on the whole thing. But I'm willing to do my part now. I want to give you a fair chance at making it succeed."

"Really?" Madison set the wreath aside.

Addie nodded. "But if it doesn't work, if we can't turn a profit, will you agree to sell?"

"Of course. It's not like we'd have much choice, would we?" Madison reached for another wreath frame.

"I guess not."

Madison really wanted to ask Addie about the books and farm finances in general but hated to ruin what felt like a real sisterly moment. That could wait until after the tree-selling season. In the meantime, she would give Addie the benefit of the doubt and try not to get her own hopes too high.

Before the evening ended, Madison not only had Addie helping with the wreaths, but Mom and Lucy, curious as to where they were, suddenly got interested too. Madison wasn't sure how long this interest would last, but for an hour, she had the three of them working on an assembly line of wreath making. And when they were done, she had enough wreaths to get them through the next day.

• • •

The next two days weren't as busy with U-cutters as Friday had been, but Madison felt relieved. She needed time to catch her breath and make more wreaths. As suspected, the three city girls lost interest in wreath making by the second evening. But Lily faithfully came and helped when she could. And Madison actually preferred the girl's company anyway.

On Sunday evening, she was just sweeping up evergreen needles and debris from the barn floor when Lucy came in. So far, Madison had barely exchanged more than a few words at a time with the young woman. But she smiled and welcomed her in. "I'm done making wreaths for the night. Well, unless you want to help?"

"Nah. I just came out for some fresh air and to poke around." Lucy sat down on one of the workbenches.

"How do you like being out here?" Madison asked as she bent to pick up the dustpan.

128

"You mean here on your tree farm?"

"Yeah, and the river in general. You know, since your dad plans to live here full-time. How do you feel about that? Not the same as what you're used to." Madison dumped the debris into the trash can.

"You can say that again." Lucy sighed. "I mean, I used to visit here sometimes. When it was the filbert farm. I guess I liked it when I was a kid. At least that's what Dad keeps telling me, but I don't really remember it."

"Well, it's a fun place for kids."

"My mom hated it."

"Oh, really?" Madison pulled out the stool across from her and sat.

"She never would've agreed to live out here in the sticks."

Madison just nodded. "Oh."

"You knew my mom, didn't you?"

"Not very well. I knew who she was, but she was a little older than me. And I didn't live here full time as a kid. Just summers and holidays."

"Well, my mom knew you." Lucy's big blue eyes seemed to bore into Madison.

"Oh, yeah, I suppose so." Madison bristled. Where was Lucy going with this?

"You were involved with my dad, weren't you?"

Madison was speechless.

"Don't worry. It's not a big deal." Although Lucy's tone suggested otherwise.

"No, of course not. That was a long time ago." Madison studied Lucy closely. "But your mom, uh, she mentioned it to you?" She felt herself fishing . . . but hadn't Lucy thrown out the bait?

"Mm-hmm."

"That's interesting. Really, I'm surprised she would even remember me."

"Oh, she remembered you, all right."

Madison studied Lucy closely. "I feel like you're insinuating something. Or maybe I'm misreading you."

"I guess I'm just curious." Lucy put her elbows on the table, folded her hands, and rested her chin on top, just staring like this was some kind of cat and mouse game.

"Curious about what?"

"Are you the reason my dad sold our nice big house and moved back here?"

Madison sat up straight. "No. Of course not. Gavin—um, your dad—didn't even know I was here. And I wasn't here then anyway. I was off in Mongolia. I only decided to come back after I heard of the fire. I wanted to help. And this place just felt like home."

Lucy continued to study her.

"It's a complete coincidence that your dad and I came back here around the same time. Well, sort of the same time."

"So you hadn't been in communication with him?"

"No." She firmly shook her head. "Not at all. I was totally surprised that he was living here."

"Well, I guess I believe you."

"I'm telling you the truth."

"So, you and Dad aren't a thing?"

"A thing?" Madison felt indignant. "We are friends. That is all."

"You don't have to get all defensive on me. I just wanted to know. And I think I have a right to know. I mean I've lost my mom and then my home and, well, it kinda felt like you were moving in on my dad."

Madison was curious to know what exactly Shelby had told her daughter, and why, but these questions would have to go unanswered. She knew to show any more interest in this conversation would only be like fuel on the fire. "Your dad is my neighbor, Lucy. And neighbors on the river help each other. And Lily has been a valuable friend to me. I hope you realize that's all it is."

Lucy's eyes narrowed slightly as her head tipped to one side. "Says you."

Madison sucked in an exasperated breath, then slowly released it.

"I happen to know that my mom sort of trapped my dad into marriage," Lucy said quietly. "It was supposed to be this deep dark secret, but Mom let the cat out of the bag a few years back. Dad was off on a business trip and Mom sort of let her hair down with me. It was pretty interesting too."

"Well, you're old enough to understand such things." Madison wanted this conversation to end. "Your mother must've trusted you enough to tell you the truth. I'm sure it was shocking, but it must've made you feel good that she'd open up—"

"She'd been drinking with girlfriends."

"Oh . . . well." Madison didn't know what to say.

"So anyway, when Mom was spilling the beans, she told me all about it. And all about you. She made it sound like you were the one Dad really loved. His first girlfriend, the girl next door, the one who got away.

"She told me how she and Dad went on this Mexico mission trip, and she made this bet with a girlfriend that she could get his attention, so she went after him in a big way. And it worked out. At least she thought so. But later on, she wasn't so sure. I mean, she never intended to get pregnant. But she even made that work for her, you know, by pressuring him into marriage."

Madison looked down at the worn worktable, tracing a deep gouge with a fingernail. She remembered hearing about that trip, remembered thinking that Gavin had forgotten her completely, had been swept away by pretty Shelby . . . and then the hasty marriage.

"So when I discovered you were here, you know, after Dad moved back. Well, you can't blame me for being suspicious, can you?"

Madison looked up, surprised to see that Lucy's eyes looked misty. "No, I can see how you might think that," she told the girl. "But I promise you, it was a total coincidence. I'll admit I've enjoyed renewing the friendship with your dad, but that's all it is." They both turned to the sound of the barn door opening.

"Oh, there you are," Addie called out cheerfully, her eyes on Lucy. "Mom and I wanna watch a good old rom-com. She wants *Sleepless in Seattle* and I want *Mama Mia*. We need a tiebreaker." She grabbed Lucy by the hand. "What say ye?"

Lucy stood. "*Mamma Mia!*, definitely."

"I knew I could count on you, girlfriend." Addie tugged her along. "Wanna join us, Madison?"

"Maybe." Madison rolled up a loose strand of ribbon. "But don't wait for me. I want to finish up in here first."

"Mom's making microwave popcorn—if she can figure it out. She already set off the smoke alarm with the first bag."

"Ooh, scorched popcorn, yum," Madison teased. "Now I'm really tempted." She followed them to the door, then latched it after they left and returned to clean the already tidy barn. She pretended to sweep but knew she was simply buying time, attempting to replay and process all that Lucy had just dumped on her. It was a lot to take in.

18

The next week Madison fell into a comforting routine. She spent most of her days outside, wearing Grandpa's old red-checked Filson jacket and using his old tractor to pull out Christmas tree stumps. She wanted to prepare the ground for the next planting. Hopefully in the spring. On days the weather was bad, she'd hole up in the barn making wreaths and garlands. On most days, Lily popped in after school to help with the wreaths, creating some very interesting ones too.

When they felt their inventory was sufficient, they decided to make the place look even more festive by hanging Christmas lights all around. Lily had unearthed several boxes of light strings in the loft. The same ones Grandpa used to put out to make the property cheery and bright. After they strung them on the barn and house, they cut down a tree that was too tall for most homes. Madison tied it to the back of the ATV and transported it to a spot beside the camping trailer. While Gavin was inside and unaware, they quietly set up the tree and strings of lights. It was just getting dusky when Lily plugged it in. They both stepped back to admire it. Against the deep blue sky, it was magically stunning. Lily knocked loudly on the door to the trailer, then they both ducked behind the tree to hide, trying not to giggle. A surprised Gavin emerged.

"Ho ho ho." He gave a hearty Santa impression. "Looks like my elves have been at work out here."

Lily popped out from behind the tree. "Do you like it, Dad?"

"I love it, honey. Thank you!"

"It was Madison's idea." Lily grabbed her hand and tugged her into view.

"I thought we needed to make your place more Christmassy." Madison grinned at the fifteen-foot-tall tree. "And we figured it might be too crowded in your trailer."

"That's for sure. Can I express my gratitude by cooking you gals dinner tonight?"

"Oh, that's not necessary." Madison waved a hand.

"But I just happened to get three beautiful T-bone steaks today. I was going to fire up the grill." He looked up at the cloudy sky. "Hopefully the weather will cooperate."

"Come on," Lily urged her. "Eat dinner with us. I'll set the picnic table."

"Only if I can bring something. I have pasta salad already made up at home. How about if I bring that over?"

"Perfect." Gavin smiled. "I'll start the charcoal."

"And I'll be right back," she promised.

When she returned, the picnic table was set, complete with a tablecloth and oil lanterns. "This looks wonderful, Lily." Madison set her bowl on the table. "So fun." She sniffed the air. "And those steaks smell fabulous."

"Almost ready. And I grilled a few veggies too," Gavin called over his shoulder.

"A December barbeque. It's a first for me." Madison helped herself to a potato chip, then sat down by the crackling campfire. By now it was dark, but that only made the lights on the Christmas tree that much prettier.

Dinner was perfect. The people, the setting, the conversation, the food—it was one of the sweetest meals Madison could remember. But as they were finishing up, big fat raindrops began to splat down.

"Let's get these things inside." Gavin began to gather plates and bowls. The three of them scrambled to grab everything, but by the time they got in the trailer, they were all rather damp. Madison piled some dishes in the sink, then looked around. She'd never been inside before. It was surprisingly nice.

"This place is roomier than I imagined." Madison took in the sofa and recliners and big-screen TV. "All the comforts of home."

"Yeah, the slide-outs make it bigger." Lily explained how they went in and out.

"Have a seat." Gavin pointed to one of the recliners. "I'll make a fresh pot of coffee."

"It's actually pretty cozy in here." She peeled off her soggy jacket and sat down. "And comfy too."

"It's better than tent camping, that's for sure."

"And I have my own space," Lily told her. "Two bunks. One for my junk. And one to sleep in."

"And a desk for homework," her dad pointed out. "As in, *hint hint*."

"Yeah, yeah."

"You get started and I'll make you a cocoa," he told her.

After Lily got her cocoa and Gavin gave Madison a mug of coffee, he sat down. "I wouldn't want to live in this trailer forever, but for the time being, it's just fine."

"The way Lucy described it, I thought it would be unbearable with three people."

"I originally thought Lucy could take one of the bunks. Of course, she wasn't having that."

Madison just smiled.

"I hope she's not too much of a burden to you."

"Oh, not at all. I think Addie loves having her around. My mom too. In fact, I'm sure they'd trade me for Lucy."

"Not really." He frowned.

"No, not really. But Lucy seems to fit into their lives better than I do."

"Or maybe they just don't fit into yours."

She sipped her coffee. "That's true. In fact, despite Addie improving her attitude, she still hints about selling the farm in the spring. I know she wants out."

"Where does your mom stand on it?"

"Well, she doesn't really have a say. Addie and I both own half. Mom's just a bystander, but I'm sure she thinks it's ridiculous to try to bring it back now. She never approved of Dad returning to help his parents."

"Reminds me of how Lucy feels about me being here."

"Fantastical dream chasers?"

"Uh-huh." He sighed and sipped his coffee.

They visited for a while, then things got quiet and Madison realized it was getting late. "I better get back." She got up and put her coffee mug in the sink.

"I'll drive you." He handed her jacket to her. "It's still raining out there."

The rain continued to pour down as he drove her home. In front of her house, which glowed prettily despite the rain, she thanked him once again for the perfectly delightful dinner, and he thanked her for the beautiful tree. Then she got out and dashed up onto the porch, pausing there to watch him pull around the circular drive and go home.

"Have a nice evening?" Addie asked from somewhere on the shadowy porch.

Madison jumped. "Holy cats! I didn't realize anyone was there. What're you doing out on such a wet night?"

"It's dry up here on the porch. I wanted to see the lights in the dark. They look nice. Good job." Addie's tone sounded flat as Madison approached the front door. "Mom said you had dinner with Gavin tonight."

"Gavin and Lily." She explained how it was his thank-you for the tree.

"That was nice. But I'm curious, was it more than that? Just a thank-you dinner? Or is something going on?"

"Nothing but neighborly friendship," Madison assured her. So maybe she was wishing it was something more. But it wasn't disingenuous to call it just friendship. That's all it was. "My jacket's still wet from the rain and it's getting late," she told Addie. "I want to get inside." She hurried in and up the stairs, going straight to her room to avoid having to explain herself to anyone else tonight.

•　•　•

The next weekend was too soggy to encourage U-cutters, but during the week, the weather improved. Despite being caught up with wreath making, Madison used her free time to pull stumps and mulch the new trees. And when Lily got home from school, the two of them went dirt bike riding, creating new trails on the Thompsons' property and even exploring some other trails. With her newfound confidence in handling her bike, Madison realized how much she loved the thrill of the ride.

Today's ride along the river trail had been the best. As usual, Madison cleaned off her bike afterward before taking it into the barn to recharge. She was just finishing when Lucy came strolling up to her. It was rare to see this girl outside of the house, but maybe the late afternoon sunshine had enticed her.

"I didn't know grown women rode dirt bikes," Lucy said in a snarky tone.

"You should try it sometime," Madison challenged as she wiped the shiny fender dry. "It's pretty fun."

"I *have* tried it." Lucy turned up her nose. "I hated it. Noisy, dirty, and the helmet gives me a headache."

"I guess it's not for everyone."

"So are you telling me you honestly like it? Or are you just doing it to impress my dad? Or maybe you think the more attached you become to Lily, the more it'll endear you to him."

Madison bristled, silently counting to ten to calm herself down. Between Lucy and Addie and her mom, she was more than fed up with catty judgments. Whether they were critiquing a less-than-glamorous contender on a *Bachelor* rerun or complaining about the mud or the food or the washing machine, it seemed there was always something wrong with something or someone. She cleared her throat and stood up straight. "I ride my bike because I enjoy it. Not everyone likes the same things, Lucy. For instance, I like to get up early. I like being outside." She held up her hands. "I like getting my hands dirty."

"Right . . ." Lucy lifted one eyebrow.

"And there are things you enjoy that I don't. So viva la différence, okay?"

"Okay." Lucy actually backed away now.

"Look, I'm not trying to offend you, but I really don't enjoy your insinuations, you know, that I'm chasing after your dad."

"Fine. I get it." Lucy's tone sharpened. "But FYI, I'm not the only one who thinks that."

Madison couldn't control her eye roll. Lucy was obviously referring to Addie. That wasn't surprising either since Addie had been going to great lengths to be around Gavin lately, taking him "homemade" cookies that she'd gotten from a bakery and set on a plate, inviting him for dinners of take-n-bake pizzas, and using every opportunity to get his attention.

"Can I speak candidly with you?" Madison asked cautiously.

"Sure. Why not?"

"Well, I know you love your father, Lucy, but how would you feel if he did find someone to be happy with? You don't expect him to remain single the rest of his days, do you?"

"No, of course not." Lucy folded her arms across her chest.

"But you'd prefer he found someone, well, more like your mother?"

Lucy brightened. "Yeah. That'd be cool."

"Maybe someone like Addie?"

"I wouldn't mind if they got together. I mean, if they were in love."

"So what you really want is to reestablish your old status quo? Perhaps your dad would give up his river dreams and go back to city living? Like when your mom was alive? Would that make you happy?"

"I wouldn't mind." Lucy's countenance faded as she gazed down at the ground, scuffing the toe of a pretty boot into a lodged stone before she looked up again. "I'm not stupid. I know I can't turn back the clock. But life really was good back then. I mean, for the most part."

Madison just nodded, holding her tongue.

"I know you think I'm selfish." Lucy pulled her faux fur–trimmed cardigan more snugly around her.

"I think you just want things to be like they were before." Madison's tone softened. "I actually know how that feels. I often wish my dad and grandparents were still alive. I wish we could all live here happily together. Just like that old TV show *The Waltons*." She smiled sheepishly. "Corny but true. Anyway, I've learned that the only constant about life is that it constantly changes. We have to adapt. Make the best of it. That's what I'm trying to do, Lucy. It's not always easy."

Lucy's eyes glistened. "Yeah, it's not."

"I remember being your age and feeling kind of lost." Madison sighed. "Sometimes I still feel kind of lost."

Lucy nodded. "Yeah. That's how I feel *all* the time."

"I don't have any great advice except what my grandma always told me. It's actually something Jesus said in the Bible. Basically, you can only live one day at a time. He said not to worry about tomorrow because today has enough problems. Just do your best here and now. Let the future take care of itself."

"Thanks, Madison." Lucy almost smiled. "I apologize for being such a royal pain."

"You're not really a pain." Madison patted her back. "But you've probably had some pain."

With pursed lips, Lucy nodded. "I think I'll go look at the river now. Dad keeps telling me to go down and see how pretty it looks. I haven't seen it once since I got here."

"It's a perfect day for it. There's a good thinking bench down there. My grandpa built it." She pointed to the tall firs. "Just past those trees. Follow that path and you'll find it."

• • •

Lily always came to help the U-cutters on weekends. It became her job to hang out the Open sign in the morning and then she'd help Madison assist customers all day Saturday and after church on Sunday. She'd even brought matching Santa hats for her and Madison to wear. Although business was good, they hadn't equaled the post-Thanksgiving crowd yet, but Madison hoped this upcoming weekend, the last one before Christmas, would be their biggest ever. To that end, she'd run a special ad in the local papers, offering hot dogs and chili as well as cookies and drinks, for tree hunters on their last open weekend.

"It's going to be super busy tomorrow," Madison told Addie on Friday afternoon. "We could probably use some help."

Addie's mouth twitched to one side. "Well, I promised to take Mom and Lucy to do some Christmas shopping. They don't know where the best places are."

"Do you think your shopping day could wait until after the weekend? Early in the week maybe?"

"But that'd be just days before Christmas." Addie frowned.

"Yeah, and this weekend is the last chance to sell trees *before* Christmas."

"But we were going to make a day of it. Mom wanted to take us to lunch. I already made reservations."

Madison knew it was pointless. Addie's mind was made up. "Well, have a good day," she said without genuine enthusiasm. Then she went outside, got out her dirt bike, and rode around to cool off her head. Of course, Lily must've heard her because she was soon riding right alongside. And then Gavin joined them. He'd been on a few rides with them, but mostly he'd just let them have the trails to themselves.

Since Madison seemed to be leading today's adventure, she headed down the river trail. Thanks to a couple of dry days, the trail was okay. They made a full loop and finally paused at the bench by the burnt oak tree. Madison got off her bike and tugged off her helmet. Still irked at Addie, she took a deep breath and exhaled loudly.

"You okay?" Gavin asked as he got off his bike. Lily, who'd taken a side trail, was still on her way.

"Yeah. I am now." She quickly explained about tomorrow's shopping trip. "I really could've used some help. Especially taking money and running cards."

"I can do that," he offered.

Finally Lily joined them. "Do what?" she asked.

"Help with selling trees tomorrow. Madison says it'll be super busy."

"Cool." Lily nodded as she revved her engine. "It's really fun." She grinned at her dad. "Beat ya home." Then she took off, spinning dirt behind her.

Gavin grinned. "My little speedster girl."

"She sure can ride." Madison watched as Lily tore across the open ground toward their property.

Gavin stepped closer to the old oak tree, peering around its trunk until he found the old carving. "It's still here." He traced his fingers over the letters.

She felt her cheeks warm but acted oblivious as she fiddled with her helmet.

"Remember this?"

"What's that?" She put her helmet back on.

"This." He pointed to the carving.

"Oh?" She stretched to look over his shoulder, then laughed. "Imagine that. How on earth did it last all these years?"

"Even survived the fire."

"Amazing." She snapped her helmet strap. "I need to get back. Still a lot to do before the weekend. But I really do appreciate your offer to help." She smiled brightly. "See you tomorrow then."

She felt rattled and embarrassed as she rode back to the barn. A part of her had longed to acknowledge the initials on the tree trunk, and yet she'd been too tongue-tied to respond. What had been his intention? Did he want to make her feel foolish—or was he hinting at something still between them?

19

"T hat was even more fun than I expected," Gavin told Madison the next evening while Lily rode out to put the Closed sign by the road. "Can I come again tomorrow, *please*?" Madison laughed. "Absolutely!"

"And I have an idea. To celebrate our successful day, how about I take you and Lily to dinner?"

"I would love that."

"Can you be ready in, say, thirty minutes?" He grimaced. "I know that's probably unreasonable, but I'm starving. That hot dog I had for lunch is long gone now."

"I can be ready in less than thirty minutes," she assured him.

"See you then!" He took off and she hurried into the house and raced up the stairs. She took a look in her mirror and was slightly horrified. Her hair was frizzy from the moist air, her old sweatshirt had a stain in front, and as she tugged off her work boots, she realized her socks were mismatched. Not that anyone could see those. But it reminded her that she wasn't exactly a fashionista. Something Addie, Lucy, or her mom would gladly point out if they got the chance. She freshened up and put on her good black jeans and a burgundy turtleneck. Then she heard voices downstairs. The women were home. She grabbed her best wool coat and hurried down.

"How'd the tree-selling business go?" Addie asked as she set down some shopping bags.

"Fabulous." Madison beamed at them. "How was shopping?"

"Exhausting." Mom sank onto the chair by the door and kicked off her stylish ankle boots. "But good."

"Well, see you later." Madison hurried out the door before they could question her. She was barely on the porch when she spied Gavin's SUV coming up the driveway. But from her vantage point, she couldn't see Lily. Gavin got out and she noticed how dapper he looked in a dark sweater and gray slacks, making her glad she had spruced up a bit. He played the gentleman by opening the passenger door for her.

"Where's Lily?" she asked as she got in.

"She begged off. Said she just wanted to stay home and relax. She was already watching a movie."

"Really?"

He shrugged. "Seemed happy to have the place to herself for a change."

When Madison reached for her seat belt, she noticed three somewhat grim, or maybe just curious, faces staring out the front room window. She turned away, focusing on Gavin as he slid in behind the wheel. His smile broadened as he really looked at her.

"You clean up well."

She snickered. "It didn't take much to improve things. I didn't realize I was such a hot mess today."

He looked surprised as he pulled out. "A beautiful hot mess."

She touched her still slightly wild hair. "Well, thanks, I guess."

"And you look extra beautiful tonight."

She took in a steadying breath. "That's really sweet of you to say that, but appearance has never been my strong suit."

"Are you kidding?"

"Not at all. My mom and Addie have always had the looks."

"Admittedly they're all attractive women, Madison, but not in your league."

She couldn't help but laugh.

"I mean it." He took his eyes off the road and glanced at her briefly. "I suppose that's just part of your beauty. Not knowing it."

She shook her head in wonder. When he turned back to the road, she studied him more closely. Was it her imagination or did he look extra handsome tonight? Maybe someone had put a spell on both of them. She felt surprisingly merry now and decided to erase the image of her three stylish housemates and their expressions of disapproval back at the house. She would not let them spoil this evening for her.

• • •

Gavin couldn't have picked a better place for dinner. And although she tried not to dwell on it too much, this felt like a very romantic date.

"I've always loved the River Inn," she told him as they were walking out to the car afterward. "It was better than ever tonight."

"The new owners have really done it up right," he said as they paused on the deck overlooking the river.

"I haven't been here since I was a kid." She leaned against the railing, gazing out over the river and admiring how the string of white lights behind them twinkled reflectively on the rippling water. "And that was only for special occasions. But it's so much nicer now. The food and everything—it was just perfect. Thanks so much for bringing me."

"I hope you don't mind that it was just the two of us."

"I'm okay with that," she said carefully. "If you are."

"This feels a little like a date to me." His tone was uneasy. Did he regret bringing her here?

She suddenly felt awkward. Had she overblown this evening in her mind? A nervous giggle escaped, which was so out of character she stood up straighter and took a deep breath. "Well, two friends sharing a meal doesn't have to make it a date, does it?" She knew her tone sounded too sharp.

"Oh?" He turned to face her now, standing so close she imagined she could feel his warmth through her heavy wool coat. "I haven't been on a real date in ages," he said quietly. "I don't even know how to act on a date anymore."

She felt herself melting. "So are you saying this is a real date?"

He looked into her face. "Would you mind if it was?"

She shook her head. And just like that he kissed her. Not a long, lingering kiss but a gentle kiss that sent a happy shiver all through her. That settled it. This was a real date. And she didn't mind a bit. He held her close.

"I've been waiting to do this," he whispered. "I hope it's okay."

"It's more than okay," she murmured. And then they shared a few more kisses, just as warm and passionate as the ones so many years ago. And for a long moment, they just embraced without speaking. She now had much more than a teenage crush going on. She wasn't even sure how to describe it. A mature familiarity . . . a connected wholeness . . . security. She was at home.

Without letting her go, Gavin stepped back to look at her. "Well, this has all been totally amazing, Madison, but I don't like leaving Lily home alone for too long."

"No, of course not."

"Although I suspect she planned this whole thing." He chuckled.

"Cupid Lily?"

"I wouldn't be surprised." With an arm still around her, he walked her to his SUV and then helped her in. She felt her heart fluttering similar to when she was a teenager, but there was something more too. Even with her pulse racing and a giddiness inside, there was stability as well, a sense of coming home.

"My girls aren't used to the idea of their dad being interested in a woman. Besides their mother, I mean. So it might be awkward for them to see me actually dating someone."

"I know."

"Of course, you already have Lily's approval. But Lucy might be a challenge."

"If it makes you feel any better, Lucy has already expressed her opinions to me."

"Seriously?" He glanced at her. "What did she say?"

"We actually had a really sweet talk. I mean, it was difficult at first." She told him about Lucy's hopes that Gavin would find a woman similar to Shelby.

"Like Addie?" he suggested.

"Exactly. It's like those two are joined at the hip."

"Maybe she can start calling her *Aunt* Addie." He chuckled, but Madison caught her breath. Was he already talking about marriage? Was she even ready for that? This was moving so fast . . . and yet her heart was singing.

At the house, he got out and walked her up to the porch. "I don't want to keep you late," he said. "But I would like a proper good night."

She glanced toward the windows. "We might be being watched."

"Let them watch. I don't care." He dramatically swooped her into his arms, making them both laugh, then landed a big kiss on her lips. And another. When he finally released her, she felt slightly dizzy . . . but happy.

"Good night, Gavin," she whispered.

"Good night, Madison." He kissed her forehead. "See you tomorrow. You don't open for business until noon, right?"

"Right. That way I can go to church."

"Yes, I've noticed you there. That's nice."

"Lily's the one who talked me into going again. I used to go with my grandparents when I was a girl."

"I know."

She smiled at him. "We have similar roots, don't we?"

"In so many ways, yes."

"We can give you a ride tomorrow."

Madison glanced at the house. "Maybe I should get there on my own. Less questions for both of us to answer."

"I'm ready to answer some questions," he told her. "Aren't you?"

She considered this. "Okay. I guess so."

He kissed her again and she opened the door. Despite her sense of foreboding, her steps felt light as she crept inside. When she heard the rustling sound of someone in the front room, she knew they'd been spied on. But like he'd just told her, *let them watch*. Why should she care? And maybe she didn't. Well, not much anyway.

• • •

Madison didn't think it was her imagination that she got the cold shoulder the next morning. She was relieved that no one was talking to her. And after grabbing some toast and coffee, she eagerly ran out the door when she saw Gavin's SUV pull up. She didn't bother asking anyone to go to church with her since they'd all turned her down last time. But maybe she could entice them to attend the Christmas candlelight service tonight. Hopefully they would thaw out before long. Otherwise it was going to be a cold Christmas. And she wasn't thinking about the weather, although there was a definite nip in the air and the forecast called for dropping temperatures.

Gavin, Lily, and Madison managed to serve the numerous U-cutters all afternoon, but by the time Lily put up the Closed sign for the last time of the season, Madison was exhausted. "That was fun, but I'm so glad it's over."

"Me too," Gavin said. "We might want to consider hiring more help next year."

"Next year?" She glanced at him, wondering more about his use of *we* than *next year* but not wanting to go there just yet.

"Well, you're not going to give up on this place, are you?"

"I don't want to. But it depends on Addie."

He nodded. "Right. I get that."

"It's getting cold out." She shivered, pulling her scarf more snugly around her neck.

"Lily is certain it'll snow by Christmas."

"That would be something." She tipped her head toward the house. "Why don't you and Lily come in for dinner? I'm not sure what I'm fixing, but I can whip up something."

"I believe it." He grinned.

"Might be spaghetti again."

"I loved that." He linked arms with her. "How about some help? I'm pretty handy in the kitchen." He waved to Lily, calling her into the house. "I bummed a meal for us."

Madison playfully jabbed him with her elbow. "I invited you and you know it."

Finding the kitchen already occupied with Mom and Addie attempting to cook and Lucy looking on, Madison wasn't sure what to do.

"I was going to make spaghetti," she told her mom.

"Too late. I'm making lasagna. There's enough for everyone. And Addie is fixing some dessert."

"Lasagna? You know how to make lasagna?" Madison blinked.

"You mean without poisoning everyone?" Mom said wryly.

"They're *premade* frozen lasagnas," Addie clarified. "One vegetarian, one not so much."

"Wow, that sounds good." Madison exchanged glances with Gavin. "Looks like we're not needed in here."

"How about I make a fire in that big fireplace out there," he suggested.

"Perfect." She nodded eagerly.

"Dinner will be ready in about forty minutes," Mom called after them. "I thought it'd be sooner, but *someone* forgot to turn on the oven."

As Madison trailed Gavin into the front room, she could hear her sister and mom arguing. Lily, bless her heart, sounded like she was trying to referee. Like that was possible.

"By the way," Madison called over her shoulder. "Don't forget that *I'm* cooking Christmas dinner this year. And it'll be ham, not turkey."

"That's a relief," Gavin told her. He was already stacking kindling in the big stone fireplace. "I guess I'm assuming we're invited."

"Don't be silly. Of course you're invited." She poked his shoulder.

"I was hoping." He lit some twisted newspaper and blew on it to ignite the kindling. "This is such a great house for Christmas." He stood and looked around with an approving expression. "Are these your grandma's decorations? I think I recognize some."

"Yes." Madison didn't want to confess the way her family had argued about using the old-fashioned decorations. Mom wanted to order fancy pieces from some swanky catalogue but fortunately discovered it was too late for delivery. Addie wanted to go shopping at Pottery Barn, but Madison finally convinced both of them that using these decorations would be cheaper and easier than buying all new stuff and starting over. And, even though she'd been tired, she'd volunteered to put them up herself when they suddenly lost interest. But Lily had helped and now it felt like homecoming to her.

"Only one thing is wrong." Gavin rubbed his beard.

"What's that?" She looked around. She hadn't put up all of Grandma's things, but that would've taken until New Year's.

"The tree."

She laughed. "Oh, we never put that up until *after* U-cut season."

"Then it's time."

She nodded. "It is."

"Do you have one all picked out?"

"I do."

His eyes twinkled. "Want to do it?"

"Tonight?" she asked.

"No time like the present."

"Are you going to cut your Christmas tree tonight?" Lily asked eagerly as she emerged from the kitchen.

"Why not?" Madison grinned. "We can take flashlights. I know the tree I want."

So the three of them bundled back up and trudged outside. They spotted the right tree, then Gavin began to saw into the trunk, with Lily and Madison aiming their flashlights for him.

He was about halfway through when Lily let out a happy shriek. "It's snowing!"

"No way." Gavin stood.

"I felt a flake on my nose," Lily told him. "Honest, I did."

"I don't believe it." He returned to sawing.

Then Madison felt a cold dampness on her cheek. She pointed her flashlight into the air. "She's right, Gavin. It is snowing."

"It's going to be a white Christmas." Lily was dancing about, her light bouncing all around, illuminating the few flying flakes in the black sky.

"Don't count your snowflakes before they stick," Gavin warned in a good-natured tone. "And please keep your lights down here if you don't mind. I don't want to cut off a finger."

With lights aimed, the tree fell, and it wasn't long before they got it up onto the porch and into the stand that Madison had ready and waiting. Gavin took the heavy end and Lily took the light end, and with Madison directing, they carried it into the house and set it into the usual place by the front window.

"It's so beautiful." Lily's eyes were wide. "I thought it would be too tall."

"I'd already measured it." Madison smiled at the noble fir. "Grandpa would be proud. Perfect shape and size and coloring and everything."

"And it smells amazing." Gavin breathed in deeply. "Nothing like the aroma of evergreen inside a house."

"Even after working the trees all day," Madison said quietly, "I still love the fresh scent." She smiled at Gavin. "Thanks for encouraging me to do this tonight. And for helping."

They were just putting colorful light strands on the tree when

Mom announced that the lasagna was done. Madison longed for some holiday peace as they came to the dining table. But she knew the three women now taking their seats were uneasy about what they suspected was developing between her and Gavin. So far no one had said a word. But it felt like a ticking time bomb. Mom attempted some polite conversation as she dished out lasagna squares, but Addie and Lucy remained cool and distant.

Madison tried to ignore their chilliness, focusing her conversation on their plans for Christmas. "I've been so distracted with the tree business that I haven't really given much thought to holiday preparations. But I plan to go into town tomorrow morning to get groceries and all that," she said to no one in particular. "I thought we could do it like Grandma always did. A light buffet on Christmas Eve and the big dinner on Christmas Day."

"Sounds good to me," Gavin said.

"Can I go with you?" Lily asked eagerly. "To town, I mean. I need to do some shopping."

"Sure." Madison smiled. "I'd love the company."

"I'd go too," Gavin said, "but I have a ten o'clock Zoom appointment. After that I hope to be free until after the New Year."

"So you say," Lily teased.

"I plan to leave my phone off," he told her.

They continued to visit pleasantly, discussing whether or not the snow, which was still lightly falling, would stick around and whether or not they should plan a trip to the mountains to see some real snow. Meanwhile the other end of the table grew even frostier. Hopefully the women would thaw out by Christmas. Because, thanks to last night, Madison had great expectations for the holidays this year. It could be her best Christmas ever. Or it could be a real heartbreaker.

20

Madison's first errand on Monday was to go to the bank. Although Addie had protested it, Madison insisted on personally depositing all the funds from the tree sales. It was an impressive sum and Madison just wanted to enjoy the process of taking it in herself. Thanks to the way Grandma had arranged the account after Dad died, Madison was a cosigner.

After she made her deposit and got a receipt that showed the balance of the account, she was surprised at the total—the farm seemed to be healthier than Addie had alluded. While still standing there, Madison requested a statement for the past six months.

"We can email that to you," the clerk told her. "Just fill out this form."

Madison filled out the form, but as she drove to the specific mall Lily had asked to go to, she felt conflicted. On one hand, she was glad to see the farm was doing better than she expected, but on the other hand, she wondered why Addie was making it seem worse. Of course, Addie wanted out and wanted to convince Madison they were in the red. But how did she plan to explain the bank account?

"We'll save grocery shopping for last," Madison told Lily as she searched for a parking place at the craft and antique mall. "Can you believe how busy it is?"

"Yeah. Think the stores will still have anything left?"

Madison laughed. "I'm sure they will. Are you looking for anything in particular?"

"I want to get Dad an antique barometer."

"An antique barometer?" Madison blinked. "Really?"

"Yeah. He's always talking about this one that burned up in the fire. It was his grandpa's and was kinda special, I guess. I'm always telling him he can check that stuff on his phone, but he really wants an old one."

"I remember that barometer, Lily. It hung in the dining room of his house."

"Cool! Maybe you can help me find one."

"Might be . . . well, hard to find." Madison wanted to say "completely impossible" but didn't want to dash Lily's hopes completely.

"I see a space over there." Lily pointed to the next row. "And it's near the antique shops. That's where I want to look."

Soon they were parked and perusing one antique shop after the next. Madison had described the old barometer as best she could recall, but so far, they hadn't found one exactly like it.

Just when they thought they'd never find one, Madison spotted something on the wall. "Hey, Lily, this is the closest thing I've seen yet." She pointed out the long narrow strip on top with the thermometer and the barometer's round gauge below.

"That's nice." Lily nodded.

"The wood seems darker, but for all I know, it could be its twin." Madison admired the antique. "Wood does darken with age."

"I like it." Lily picked it up, looked at the price, then frowned. "But it's more than I wanted to pay."

"I wonder if you can haggle."

"Haggle?"

"Talk them down on the price. People did that all the time in Mongolia. It was just the normal way to buy things."

"Okay." Lily picked the barometer up again. "I'll go haggle."

"Good luck. I'll keep looking around." Madison had already found a few interesting pieces that would make good gifts. Well, *she* thought they'd be good. It remained to be seen what her mom and sister would think. She'd even gotten an old dartboard set that Lily had fallen in love with, sneaking it out to her Jeep while Lily was at the other end of the shop. But she'd yet to find anything for Gavin.

Lily's haggling, plus her preteen enthusiasm, worked like a charm. She got the price down even lower than hoped. As they went to the car, Madison confessed she was having trouble finding something for Gavin.

"You used to know my dad when you were kids, right?" Lily asked as she laid her carefully wrapped treasure in the back seat.

"Right."

"What kind of things did he love back then?"

Madison tried to think as she got in the car. "Well, life was pretty simple. I mostly saw him in the summertime. Of course, he loved his old pickup. Can't afford one of those." She laughed. "Mostly we loved good times on the river."

"And he's already got the river."

"Rafting!" Madison exclaimed. "He had this old rubber raft. I think it was his dad's. Big yellow stinky thing. We used to shoot the rapids in it. It was a blast."

"That sounds awesome. Get him one of those."

Madison frowned as she started the Jeep. "Yeah, good idea. Where do I find a yellow rubber raft in wintertime?"

"Can I see your phone?" Lily asked.

Madison handed it to her, watching as the girl did a quick internet search and then called a number. "Do you have yellow rubber rafts?" she asked. Satisfied with the answer, she directed Madison to a sporting goods store, and before long, they were hefting a box holding a yellow rubber raft into a cart, as well as a pair of paddles.

"This is great," Madison said as together they lifted it into the back of the Jeep. "Perfect."

"Will you wrap it and put it under your tree?"

"Of course." Madison laughed. "But I better get more wrapping paper. I noticed my grandma's supply was getting thin."

"I bet it'll be the biggest thing under the tree."

By the time they'd finished shopping, had a quick lunch, and had gotten groceries, it was past two. But Madison felt all set for Christmas. Only one thing bothered her. What about the farm's business account? She knew she should wait until after Christmas to bring it up, but it was gnawing at her now. She dropped off Lily and was about to leave when Gavin came out to help unload Lily's packages.

"Want to go with us to the candlelight service on Christmas Eve?" he asked Madison.

"I'd love to go. I hope Mom will too. I don't know about Addie though. She's been a little antichurch in adulthood. But maybe I can remind her of how much she liked the candlelight service as a little girl." Madison sighed. "Our grandparents took us, and we both always loved the candles and singing and everything."

"So did Lucy," Gavin said eagerly. "Maybe you can encourage her too. I already asked, but she just rolled her eyes at me." He looked wistfully at Madison as Lily went inside the trailer. "It'd be so great to have all our family members there for Christmas Eve."

"I know. I'll try, but I'm not sure they'll listen to me," she confessed. "We don't see eye to eye on a lot of things."

"Just do your best." He kissed her on the cheek, sending a fresh rush of happy nerves through her. "And we'll both pray about it, okay?"

"Definitely."

After she got home and put things away, she went online to check the business account and grew even more perplexed. Something was really wrong here. Unable to keep her concerns to herself, she decided to just get this mess out in the open. After finding out from her mom that Addie was holed up in her office, Madison marched out of the house and knocked loudly on the door.

"Leave me alone" was the curt answer.

Madison flung open the door to find her sister in her cozy little haven, curled up on the sofa with the TV on. "Working hard?" Madison walked into the overly warm and stuffy space.

"I came in here to be alone." Addie muted the TV. "Can't you take a hint?"

Leaving the door ajar, Madison sat in the desk chair and gazed around. Not for the first time, she noticed this was a pretty posh little office. Money had been spent in here. "What's going on with our business account, Addie?" she demanded. "I just saw the statement for the past six months. We are *not* in the red. In fact, we are very comfortably in the black."

"That should make you happy." Addie's lower lip protruded.

"It makes me confused." She threw her arms in the air. "How can we be doing that well?"

Addie sighed with a defeated expression.

"I want the truth, Baby Sister. *Now.*" Madison put on the same expression she'd used when babysitting Addie long ago.

"I-I planned to tell you . . . when the time was right. When it was time to sell."

"Tell me what?"

"Grandma's life insurance policy," she blurted out. "It was bigger than I let on. It was paid off to you and me last winter. You were out of reach, so the lawyer oversaw the deposit in our joint account."

Madison frowned. "You didn't want me to know so I'd think we were going under and were forced to sell?"

Addie slowly stood, her eyes brimming with tears. "I'm tired of trees. I'm done. I want out, Maddie."

Madison's heart softened at the use of her old nickname. "I know you do."

"Selling is the only way I can get my share." She sniffled.

Madison considered this. "I don't know the value of the property, but what if we made a deal? You could have most of what's already in the business account. Consider my portion of our inheritance as your down payment. And I would guarantee you a percentage of profits down the line? Like a partial owner. It would be an investment in your future. Would that help?"

She blinked. "Well, I was pretty strapped after I quit my job, you know, because of the divorce and everything. It's the main reason I was so eager to come here. I'd been hoping for a way to start over. But as we know, I'm not really an outdoorsy kinda gal."

"I know." Madison reached for her sister's hand, squeezing it. "And that's okay. You did what you could. And I appreciate how you held the farm together until I got home. Maybe this is your chance to really live your life now. Making this arrangement could make that possible, Addie. I could give you a fresh start."

"You'd really be willing to do this?" Addie's eyes were misty. "I mean, after everything I've done?"

"I'm more than willing. If it allows me to keep the farm. Of course, we'll have to get the lawyer to write it all up and make it fair."

"Absolutely." She beamed and then sighed. "I'd be free."

"With a nice nest egg to take with you."

Addie threw her arms around Madison, sobbing. "I'm sorry I've been so lousy to you, Madison. I've just been so frustrated. You were living overseas, chasing your dreams, traveling Europe. Then you come home like the hero—here to save the day. On top of everything else, Gavin likes you better than me. It's like you keep winning, and I keep getting the shaft."

"I'm truly sorry things have been so hard on you. And I really am grateful you were here with Grandma after Dad died. And how you helped her keep the farm going. That made me able to do what I did. But you really deserve your freedom now."

Addie nodded. "Maybe I'll go to Europe now."

"You should!"

They both turned to the sound of the door squeaking open. "I want to go to Europe too," Mom told them with a grin.

"Mom! You heard all that?" Addie asked with wide eyes.

"Madison looked so mad. I was afraid she might come out here and do you in," Mom teased. "I've never seen my firstborn so furious before."

"Oh, Mom." Madison frowned.

"But when I heard how you tricked her, Addie"—Mom shook a forefinger at her baby—"well, I can understand her anger. That was despicable, Addie."

"I'm not proud," she confessed.

"I'm just glad to see you girls straightening it out." Mom opened her arms. "Group hug?"

"But we're not a huggy family," Madison reminded her as she embraced them both.

"People change," Mom told her. She stepped back, straightening her silky tunic shirt. "Just don't expect miracles, okay?"

Madison smiled. "Speaking of miracles. I want you two to come to church with Gavin and Lily and me for the Christmas Eve service. And I want you to encourage Lucy to come too. Her dad really hopes she will."

They agreed. Albeit reluctantly. But when the time came, they all piled into Gavin's SUV and quietly, awkwardly rode to church together. They sat in the back and the service was simple and beautiful, and unless Madison was mistaken, everyone in the little country church felt blessed by it. The ride home was just as quiet as it had been going, but the atmosphere felt different. Madison might've been imagining it, but to her, it felt almost holy.

21

Something on the farm felt decidedly different on Christmas Day. Madison knew it wasn't her imagination now. As the household went about holiday preparations, with a steady stream of Christmas music playing in the background, some of the women volunteered their help in the kitchen, quietly slipped wrapped gifts under the tree, or fished out leftover ornaments still nestled in boxes and hung them on the few empty branches. All the while, there was a palpable sense of calm in the house. Maybe even love. Madison was afraid to mention this phenomenon to anyone or do anything to rock the boat, lest the peace evaporate.

"It's so weird that your family doesn't open gifts until after dinner on Christmas Day," Lily said as they finished setting food on the big dining table.

"It was just my grandparents' way," Madison explained for what felt like the tenth time. Poor Lily was so impatient to have gifts opened!

"She already told you," Lucy chided her younger sister.

"I know," Lily said with impatience. "It's because they used to keep the tree farm open all day on Christmas Eve."

"You'd be surprised how many people waited that long to get their trees," Madison told her. "My grandparents would close up just before dark, and then they'd be too tired to do much of anything. Not until after Christmas dinner the next day. It's just how it was done."

"And still is," Addie chimed in as she set a bowl of mashed potatoes on the table. "I kind of like it. Makes Christmas last longer."

Madison smiled gratefully at her. "Good point."

By the time they sat down for dinner, that feeling of holiday congeniality and peace left over from the night before was still present. And as Gavin said a blessing, they truly felt like one big family. Really, truly family. Madison actually felt misty-eyed as everyone said "amen."

After dinner, to Lily's delight, they gathered around the tree for the gift exchange. Lily, playing elf, happily distributed the gifts. Madison could tell she was as excited about giving the presents she'd picked out as she was about opening her own gifts.

They were nearly done with the exchange when Lily let out a happy shriek. "It's snowing," she cried out. They all went to look out the window where, indeed, a few snowflakes were fluttering down. Just lightly, but with promise of more.

Gavin loved his antique barometer from Lily, and everyone else seemed pleased with both giving and receiving. Even Mom and Addie liked the handcrafted pieces Madison had found and carefully wrapped for them. And she had to admit that their more fashionable gifts might prove good assets to her rather meager and style-challenged wardrobe.

"Now for the biggest gift under the tree." Lily tugged out the heavy box. "Who could this be for?" She read the card. "'To Gavin, from Santa.' Hmm . . . you must've been a good boy, Dad." She winked at Madison. "Although I don't think Santa is the one behind this." She scooted the big box in front of him, and everyone watched as he peeled off the paper.

"A rubber raft!" he exclaimed. "Just what I've been wanting." He looked at Madison. "You?"

She just grinned.

"You and I used to have some good times on my old raft. You remember?"

"Oh, yeah." She felt her cheeks warm to remember some of the afternoons they'd spent floating down calmer parts of the river. "I remember all right."

Gavin made an uncomfortable-sounding chuckle.

"You're blushing, Dad," Lucy teased him. "Anything you'd like to share with the group?"

"As a matter of fact." He went over to Madison and tugged her to her feet. "I would like to share something." He reached into his pocket. "We just had the biggest gift of the evening. Now we will have the smallest."

He produced a blue velvet box from his pocket, then got down on one knee. "Madison McDowell, I love you. I have loved you for a long while." He opened the box to reveal a simple but lovely diamond ring. "Will you please do me the honor of becoming my wife?"

Madison felt her jaw drop as she stared at the ring. Was this for real? Was she daydreaming? "Oh my!" she said in a hushed tone. Everyone in the room stared at them in stunned silence, expressions impossible to read. Did Gavin even realize the position he'd put everyone in? Feeling helpless and speechless and somewhat confused, she looked down at him, still balanced on one knee.

"Don't leave me hanging here," he said a bit lightly. "What do you say, Madison? I know this might seem presumptuous, but believe me, I've given it lots of thought. Will you marry me? I'm asking in front of witnesses because we're all part of this. Can you accept me and my two beautiful daughters? Can you accept us as part of your family?"

Madison glanced at Lily, who was beaming joyfully. Next she nervously turned to Lucy. To her surprise, an amused smile played upon the pretty girl's lips. Madison looked over at Mom and Addie, and although they still looked slightly shocked, they both nodded as if to give consent.

Last, Madison's gaze returned to Gavin. She caught her breath at the intensity of his dark blue eyes as he studied her. The poor guy looked even more nervous now! So she smiled down at him. "Yes, Gavin Thompson, I would love to become your wife."

Gavin's whole face lit up as he stood, and right there, in front of God and everyone, they kissed—passionately!

And everyone in the room clapped and cheered!

MELODY CARLSON is the award-winning author of more than 250 books with sales of more than 7.5 million, including many bestselling Christmas novellas, young adult titles, and contemporary romances. She received a *Romantic Times* Career Achievement Award, her novel *All Summer Long* has been made into a Hallmark movie, and the movie based on her novel *The Happy Camper* premiered on UPtv in 2023. She and her husband live in central Oregon. Learn more at MelodyCarlson.com.

Enter a world of family mysteries, royal jealousies, and happily ever afters

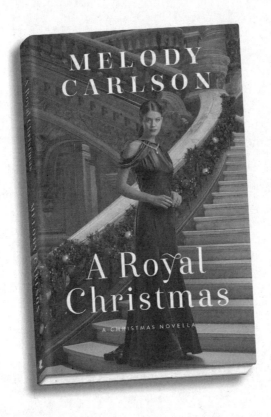

"Carlson's latest impeccably written inspirational romance is wholesome holiday fun."

—Booklist

COZY UP WITH THIS SWEET STORY *of* GIVING *and* FORGIVING

"Perfect for fireside reading
on a cold December night."
—Publishers Weekly

Fall in Love
This Christmas

Revell
a division of Baker Publishing Group
RevellBooks.com

Available wherever books and ebooks are sold.

MEET
Melody

MelodyCarlson.com